CHARLIE ELLIS

CHARLIE ELLIS
AND THE
DAY TRIP TO MARS

by Paul Sutton

Buffalo Books
Cambridge

978-1-9997231-0-1
Published by Buffalo Books, Cambridge
camerajournal@hotmail.com
10, 9, 8, 7, 6, 5, 4, 3

Also by Paul Sutton

The Old and the Young
Understanding Gary Numan
Talking About Ken Russell
Six English Filmmakers
The Lemon Popsicle Book
Lindsay Anderson, The Diaries
Becoming Ken Russell

Also by Buffalo Books

To Each His Own Dolce Vita by John Francis Lane
Falling Upwards by Tim Dry
Ken Russell's Dracula

CHARLIE ELLIS

Contents

Part One
The Day Trip to Mars
page 1

Part Two
The Philosophers
page 61

Part Three
The Seven Unconquered Planets
page 113

Preface

He had been asleep for a long time when Grandma brought him flowers. Purple roses. She said the scent would help him to dream. And he did dream. He dreamed of the lake. In the lake he could see faces, the faces of people he knew, and the face of a boy. The flowers decayed, imperceptibly at first, and the scent changed, imperceptibly. And when the scent changed, the dream changed until the sky was above him and below him. He could see treetops.

Chapter 1

Grandad and Grandma had real names, of course, but their real names didn't seem to fit so, to Charlie, they were always Grandad and Grandma. They were at what Grandad called The Twilight of Life. They had lived a lot and they had done a lot, and now, settled into a comfortable routine, they were happier than they had ever been before. Their eyesight was failing but they took daily pleasure in reading good books: "I enjoyed that," said Grandad. "It was a very good book."

Their lungs had never been weaker but they both enjoyed the quick breathlessness of long country walks: "He steams into the lead and is almost at the top!"

"Don't go running off like a fool," shouted Grandma. "It's not a race. Wait there! Let me catch up. I'm the one carrying the food." Their minds were not as quick as they used to be, memory was no longer a reliable tool, and meal times were rarely without a prescribed pill, but this didn't seem to matter. They had each other. They had their routine. Each day they rose at seven. Each night they went to bed at midnight: "There's no point in giving in until the day is done," said Grandad.

On Friday mornings, Grandma bought eggs, meat and vegetables from the farmer's market in Roeminster. On Friday evenings, in season, Grandad attended, and sometimes gave, The Village Hall

Lecture. In two week's time he would be lecturing about the Roman occupation of Roeminster. His lecture would begin: "On this very day in the year One Hundred and Three, a Roman warrior stood at the very spot on which I'm standing. And you lot, sitting here before me, would not be artists or engineers or farmers, you'd all be soldiers, centurions, men of war, all of you, except for Mr. Brown there. Mr. Brown would be a Briton. And Mr. Brown was about to be executed for plotting an insurrection."

Grandad wasn't a professional historian but he liked to read history books. The kitchen table was piled with books about Romans in Britain. Grandma would soon be telling him to clear the table. It was almost time for dinner. Then, through the steamed window, she saw Charlie. "Charlie's back!"

"Already?"

Charlie had been living with them for two years now. He was a cheerful boy with a natural ability to light up a room, but his arrival had caused Grandad's health to falter because it had brought changes to the routine. There had been new things to think about, more things to do. It had taken seven months for a new routine to settle itself and for Grandad's health to revive to its present level of a minimal decline.

Grandma, aproned, at the window, said: "Something must have gone wrong." She could see that Charlie's head was down. He was walking with a measured stride across the open field. "Poor little soul. He was so looking forward to it. I wonder what could have gone wrong?"

"Well, he's alright and that's the main thing," said Grandad. "We'll find out soon enough."

Grandma opened the back door and waited for Charlie. As she waited, she dried her hands on her apron although her hands didn't need drying. Charlie nodded a formal greeting, almost in the high German manner, and said: "Hello, Grandma... Nobody came." They went into the house.

"Nobody at all?"

"Not one," said Charlie. "So we've postponed it for a few days, until a week on Thursday, because the weather is meant to be bad at the weekend."

"What makes you think the TV people will be there on Thursday?" asked Grandad, a book in each hand.

"Well, we made a film. We flew round the Earth instead, just a quick loop, and we filmed it. Can I show you?" From his pocket he took out a disc. He held it up for them to see.

"After dinner," said Grandma. "We were just about to have dinner." She noticed that the lunch box in Charlie's other hand was full.

"I'm sorry, I forgot. I was busy," said Charlie. "I don't get hungry when I'm busy. I ate the flapjack though." She took the box from him and put it down on the sideboard as she helped him out of his coat. "I'll eat the sandwiches for dinner," said Charlie. "They won't go to waste. Couldn't I just show you a little clip? You'll like it."

"You'll eat dinner for dinner," insisted Grandma, taking the re-offered disc and turning it over in her hand.

"Just two minutes?" said Charlie.

Grandma gave him back the disc. "Put it in the machine. We'll watch two minutes."

A visitor to Grandad and Grandma's house would be surprised by the sophistication of their Home Entertainment Centre. A button on a remote control caused the whole wall on one side of the room to slide back to reveal a curved screen bigger than the one in the small cinema in town. The press of another button opened a compartment beneath the screen onto which Charlie placed the disc. The compartment closed. Grandad, Grandma and Charlie sat down in three of the four armchairs. The armchairs, with embroided covers by Grandma, were facing each other, arranged for conversation. "I like this," she said, a finger poised above the remote control. "Are you ready?"

"Ready for the butterflies," mumbled Grandad.

"It's not as bad as that," said Grandma. She pressed the button. The floor moved so that the armchairs swung into alignment facing the screen. The chairs tilted back.

"Are you ready?"

"Ready," said Charlie.

"Lights!" shouted Grandad. The lights went out. Grandma pressed another button which brought shutters down over the windows. The disc started to play a film recorded by Charlie's mobile phone. On the screen was a grassy hilltop. On the grassy hilltop was a spaceship, circular, white, the kind you would expect to see in an old science-fiction film. Standing by the spaceship was a man, Steve Atherton, a good friend of the family. Steve didn't look like a spaceman because he was wearing ordinary clothes.

"There's a consequential good taste in the plainness of his clothes," observed Grandma, in a tone which suggested she was quoting someone.

"He's wearing that jumper you gave him," said Grandad.

"It looks good on him. I knew it would. He's easy to shop for because he's slim."

"I'm slim," said Grandad.

"You're slim but you stoop."

"Stoop? Poop," said Grandad.

On the screen, Charlie walked into view; his back to the camera. "My phone's on top of a stone," said Charlie.

"It looks very professional," said Grandma.

In the film, Steve and Charlie posed for the camera, wide snap-shot smiles. Then they turned and walked to the spaceship from which an hitherto unseen door opened. A ramp descended. Steve and Charlie went inside. The ramp withdrew. The door closed. In the wait for something else to happen, Grandad opened his mouth to speak but he didn't speak. Without fuss, the spaceship lifted into the air until it was out of shot. Six seconds later it came back into shot. It landed and opened. Charlie ran out and picked up the phone, still recording, and he carried it into the spaceship. From the outside of the spaceship there didn't seem to be any windows but, from the film, you could see that inside there was an all-round view. You could see fields and hills in every direction.

"That's clever," said Grandad.

"What is?" asked Grandma.

"The fact you can see out but you can't see in."

"It's all done with cameras," said Charlie. "It films what's outside and projects it inside."

"It must be bad for your eyes."

"No, there's no motion glare," explained Charlie. "So there's no chance of motion sickness. And you can switch it off if you want to."

"How?"

"You just say 'Viewing screens off' or something like that. Almost everything is voice-activated."

"Very clever," said Grandad, stroking his chin.

By now, the unedited film was showing the view from outer space as seen from Charlie's camera phone. They could see the Earth. "Is that the Great Wall of China?" asked Grandma.

"The Andes, I think," guessed Grandad.

"We've posted copies of the disc to all the TV stations listed in the book. Well, not all of them. We sent fifty. There were only fifty jiffy bags at the post office. Mrs. Williamson didn't seem at all pleased when we bought them all."

"She is a strange woman," muttered Grandma, mostly to herself.

"The English will probably still think it's a hoax," said Grandad, "but some of the foreign stations will turn up. Have you sent it to any?"

"Erm, lots — to France, Germany, Belgium, Poland, Seattle, Italy, Japan, and Norway."

"I bet she moaned about you buying up her stamps?" complained Grandma.

"You were right to postpone it, Charlie," said Grandad. "It wouldn't do for the first manned flight to Mars to go by without independent record."

After a polite pause, Grandma pressed a button on the remote control which brought the film to a stop and which returned the room to a recognisable normality. "It's all very impressive, dear," she said, "but dinner will spoil if we leave it any longer. And you've already gone without lunch."

Chapter 2

"Describe me."

"What do you mean?"

"Describe me."

"You're small for your age."

"Am I?"

"Not really."

"You're skinny."

"No, I'm not."

"Your hair manages to be both tidy and scruffy all at the same time."

"See. I told you it was impossible."

Chapter 3

The journey started eight years ago when Charlie was five years old. His mother, over-busy with work, and needing time to herself, carried Charlie over to Steve's house, at an agreed early afternoon hour, and said: "It'll be a big help if I can have a clear four or five hours. More if you're able to. He'll eat whatever you eat. He's not a fussy eater. He'll curl into a ball and fall asleep when the sun goes down. And he wakes by the sun. You can time your clocks by him."

The boy's father was away on business. His grandparents were holidaying in East Europe.

"Hello, Charlie," said Steve.

Charlie curled into the folds of his mother's dress. "Oh, don't be silly," she chided, taking hold of the boy's right hand and holding him away from herself and towards Steve. "You know Mr. Atherton. Be a good boy. Say 'Hello'. Charlie didn't say anything but he didn't wriggle back into the dress and that was something. She said: "He likes drawing. He likes colours. He likes making patterns with colours. When he's done with drawing, maybe you could find something on TV? Call me when you've had enough. If he tantrums let him cry himself out."

Steve added a cushion to a chair so that Charlie could sit at the table. He gave him a sheet of white paper, taken from the feed tray of a printer, and he gave him a single black pen. "I don't have any colours. I've only got black pens. I'm sorry. Can you draw me something black? Something without colour?"

With a seriousness uncommon for his years, Charlie thought about the request before nodding once and saying: "Yes." Partly from shyness, partly from a lack of vocabulary, but mostly because he had an strange penchant for accuracy, Charlie's conversation, at this age, was rarely more than one or two words. Steve watched as Charlie drew small circles, on very specific points, over much of the paper. And when the circles were all in place, Charlie carefully filled them with ink, taking care to deliberately go over the edges, just a little bit. Then Charlie drew and inked a larger circle. His face was beaming when he lifted up the paper for Steve to take.

"What have you drawn?"

At first, Steve thought he was looking at an abstract drawing, a series of small black dots artfully placed, with a single large black dot to the left of the centre.

"The sky," said Charlie.

"The sky?" repeated Steve.

"Backwards," explained Charlie.

"The sky backwards?"

Charlie nodded. He had drawn a picture of the night sky. The white was black and the black was white.

"What's the big black dot?"

"The moon," said Charlie. The little dots were stars.

Steve was amazed. "Charlie, this is wonderful. Can I keep it?"

Charlie nodded.

In the years that followed, Steve thought he perceived constellations in the too-careful-to-be-random placing of the stars. "Who taught you how to draw like that? Your mother? Your father?"

Charlie didn't answer because he didn't understand the question. Steve gave Charlie another piece of paper and asked: "Please, can you draw a picture of me, standing here in this room? I'll stand very still." Charlie drew slowly and carefully, barely lifting the pen from the paper as if he was trying to complete, in a single line, the drawing of the man in his room. For all the imperfections of detail and line, the completed drawing was remarkable in that Charlie had instinctively understood the meaning of scale. The figure of the man was the right size in proportion to the room in which he was standing. The composition was sufficiently accurate to be representative, and there was more than a hint of an understanding of perspective. Steve was genuinely astonished. He said: "You're the most remarkable boy I've ever met."

Charlie smiled.

On the table in front of Charlie Ellis were architectural drawings, the plans to extend and enlarge a linked series of laboratories and work rooms that had been cut into a natural hillside cave. On the far end of the table was a surgical teaching tool, a scale model of a human head, with a cutaway skull and a removable brain. Steve said, "Can I show these drawings? They are the work rooms in the caves up from Grandad's lake. You've been there with Grandad. And we've been fishing in the lake. Do you remember? We caught three silver fishes with red fins. Grandma cooked them on a smoky fire that made your Grandad cough. Can you see the man at the entrance to the cave? The man's there to give the drawing human scale. Scale is the size of one thing in relation to another. So, as you can see, these are going to be very big rooms. These straight lines, and these numbers in the corner, are the guide lines for the architect, the builders. The men who take this idea, or ideal, and make it real. The lines have been drawn with a ruler. Have you ever used a ruler to do a drawing?"

Charlie hadn't.

"Here." Steve placed a fresh sheet of paper and a steel ruler on the table in front of Charlie Ellis. "Look closely at the ruler. Can you see the number one?"

Charlie picked up the ruler. It was heavy. He inspected it and nodded.

"What number does the ruler go up to?"

"Twelve," answered Charlie.

"And how many little lines are there in each of the twelve numbers?" Charlie could see that the twelve numbers on the ruler were broken into smaller units. He counted them aloud but quietly.

"Eight".

"Good. One of the beauties of imperial measurements is that they can be multiplied and sub-divided indefinitely and with great accuracy. If six is half of twelve, what is half of eight? You can look at the ruler to help you."

"Four."

"Good boy. What is half of eight inches and six bits? or eight point six? See if you can do it without looking."

Charlie closed his eyes and, after a thinking-pause, said: "Four and three."

"Four point Three. Good. You are a superb boy."

Charlie smiled. Steve Atherton showed Charlie how to draw a straight line using the ruler, and when the boy's ruled lines were confident, the inked lines of a smiliar thickness, Steve drew a rect-angular box on a fresh piece of paper. He marked the longer side '8 1/2' and the shorter he marked '5'. Using the ruler and the edges of the paper, Steve showed what he meant by parallel. "Side by side like train tracks. They never meet. Like obsessive scientists and a good wife. Have you been on a train?"

Charlie nodded. Steve asked him to draw the box accurately and to the correct scale. The resulting drawing was perfectly usable. "Good boy. Let's break for something to eat. Then we can carry on.

What do you want? I've got a cooked chicken, with boiled potatoes and some cabbage, and mustard. I've only got tea and water to drink. And milk. Does your mother let you have tea?"

After eating and drinking, and a washing of hands, Steve took the paper with Charlie's box drawing on it and he filled the box with a slow drawing of an electric circuit that included an oscillator and a transmitter. When the drawing was complete, he said: "Now, like the men who are going to use my drawings of the workrooms in the caves to make real work rooms, we are going to use this drawing to make a real electric circuit. Electricity is what makes the lights go on. Then, with help from an old keyboard to punch in the numbers, we'll turn the circuit into a telephone. And you'll be able to speak to your mother. We can make a speaker out of a piece of paper. It's fun. I'll show you how it's done."

Charlie smiled. They built the circuit using copper wires, small silver sheets, and a battery taken from a wristwatch. "That's the core of it anyway. Can you see how the oscillator works? It'll run forever if the calculation is right and it strikes the right balance using its own weight and gravity."

When the telephone was assembled, Charlie pressed the keyboard numbers with a studied carefulness. It worked at the very first attempt.

"Hello... Yes... Yes.... It's Charlie... Yes.... Yes..." It was 10.20pm. For the first time in his life, Charlie Ellis hadn't fallen asleep in unity with the falling sun.

Within the week, Charlie was back at Steve's house, leading a grateful mother by the hand and brandishing a drawing for Steve. His mother said: "He's been talking about you all week. He says you can make everything. He's drawn something for you to make."

Steve took the rolled drawing and, unrolling it, said: "Let's see what you want me to make for you?"

It was a drawing of a spaceship. Circular. A regular UFO. The mother departed with a grin that said 'that'll teach you'.

"It's a lovely picture," said Steve honestly. "But I don't know if I can build a spaceship, Charlie. It's a lot of work. I mean, what's the scale of this? Oh, I see. That's a robot. Is the robot the size of a man?"

Charlie nodded.

"And you've coloured the spaceship silver?"

Charlie nodded.

"Silver's a good metal," agreed Steve. "Good for conducting electricity and it's very reflective but it's brittle and expensive. I don't know whether it'll be right for a real spaceship. Perhaps it could be used in an alloy, say with titanium? Titanium is light and strong and expensive. It's what the Americans use. I suppose we could spend the afternoon testing a few metals for their strength and weight and suitability. Will that be okay for a start?"

Charlie nodded.

"If we're going to do this, we'll have to do it properly. And it won't be plain sailing. If we are going to build a working spaceship, you will have to do your fair share of the work."

Charlie nodded and smiled. And that was enough to seal the deal.

Chapter 4

Charlie was at the kitchen table eating a breakfast of toasted bread and fried eggs splashed with vinegar. Grandma was sitting across from him, enjoying his company, and turning a blind eye to the brief slips of manner brought on by the excitement of the day. But she wasn't prepared to let out-and-out rudeness go unchecked.

"Charlie!"

"Sorry, Grandma." He took his elbows off the table.

"I hope you remember your manners when you're with Mr. Atherton?"

"Yes. He's as strict as you are."

"Good."

"And I have to behave because of the cameras."

"Cameras?"

"Everything inside and outside the ship is recorded by cameras, for safety reasons as well as for science ones. And everything is beamed back to Earth for you to see on TV. And it's all voice-activated,

'Lights on. Heating up. Screens on. Cameras off', even the new security system."

"Security?"

"System. You know what it's been like these last few days, with all the reporters and helicopters and everything? If anyone enters the spaceship who isn't registered, it seals itself and knocks them out."

"Knocks them out?"

"By removing the oxygen if they're on their own, or by electricity if they're not. A real thunderbolt thing, with a whip-crack sound and everything."

"I don't like the sound of that," said Grandma. "Does Grandad know about this?"

"It's perfectly safe, Grandma."

"How does it know *you* are *you*?"

"Because of my voice patterns," explained Charlie. "And my weight, and because of the blink of my eye. I do the iris-blink-wink, like this." Charlie leaned forward and did the iris-blink-wink for Grandma then he forked in a too-large mouthful of food. The extended period of chewing allowed a natural lull in the conversation to be filled by the noise of a helicopter passing over-head. Charlie and his grandma looked up and followed the noise across the ceiling and out across the open field.

"If they find the Bat Cave," said Charlie, which was the name he'd given to Steve's workrooms, "and get into it, and someone gets into the ship and tampers with it, it could be a disaster. And if anyone tries to touch the ship they'll be electrocuted."

"What!"

"The spaceship electrocutes them."

"What?"

"Steve's built an electric field around it strong enough to knock out an ox."

"Charlie?"

"That's just how it is. It won't knock us out because our fingertips have been programmed in. You can have yours done if you want to?"

"What if you lean against it with a shoulder?" asked Grandma. "Will the finger-tipping work then?"

"It's only a temporary thing, a security thing."

"You're talking with your mouth full again, Charlie."

"Sorry."

"Mr. Atherton wants you there at ten o'clock. Have you had enough to eat?"

"Yes, thanks," said Charlie, catching the last bits of food with repeated scrapes of his knife and fork.

"Well, it's time. Give me a kiss, then get yourself gone."

"Just let me finish chewing this."

With a smiling thoroughness, Charlie chewed the last mouthful of food. "And let me finish my swig."

Swig was the name Charlie and Steve gave to any drink that wasn't tea or milk. He downed a half glass of water in three cleaning gulps. He wiped his mouth with his hand and he gave Grandma a kiss. She held him close.

"You're the most important thing on the trip, Charlie Ellis. Never forget that. You're more important than any sights you see or any discoveries you make. You're more important than Science itself."

"More important than Steve?"

"To us you are, and to him." She released him from her grip. From a kitchen cupboard, Charlie took a carrier bag into which he placed his sandwich box and a bottle of water. Then he put on his coat. He thought about fastening it but chose to leave it unbuttoned. He kissed Grandma goodbye.

In the garden, Grandad was pushing a wheelbarrow filled with grass cuttings. He stopped to shake Charlie's hand. "Are you nervous?"

"Not really," said Charlie, truthfully.

"If the trip is successful there'll be a lot of changes around here. Tourists, well-wishers, crackpots. You've become very famous this week and things can only get worse. But don't worry. Plans are in place to keep you safe. When you get back, keep your head up and keep your feet on the ground and everything will be all right."

"Yes, Grandad."

"Good. You're a good lad, Charlie Ellis." He ruffled Charlie's hair. Charlie smiled. Grandad continued: "I saw Cedric this morning. He's a bit concerned by the size of the crowd on Horsepool Hill, but the police seem to have things under control. Everyone will want to crowd you and question you but remember you are not obliged to answer all their questions. It's best not to answer anything too personal, what you give away is taken away, but it is important too not to be impolite. In public life, there's a fine line between rudeness and acceptance, and that's a line you'll have to find all by yourself."

"Yes, Grandad."

"About the trip, keep your thinking head on at all times. I know Mr. Atherton will have prepared for all possibilities, but your personal safety is your personal responsibility. Never forget that. See as much as you can. Learn as you much as you can. And enjoy yourself."

"Yes, Grandad."

"You'll be back when? In a week?"

"Yes. Maybe eight days if the weather on Mars isn't good."

"We'll look forward to having you back. And we'll watch you on the television, of course. We'll tune in as often as we can."

Chapter 5

Charlie walked the two-thirds of a mile across open gorsewood fields until he came to a dense woodland crossed with hidden paths. The first path led to the first oak. The second path to the second oak. The third led to an oak tree that was not an oak tree at all. Behind it a rock rolled away to reveal a steel and stone antechamber into the floor of which had been cut a hole the size of a double manhole cover. Rising out of the hole, and now locking into the ceiling, was a fireman's pole. Charlie gripped the pole with his hands and knees and slid down. At the bottom, he typed a curious sentence into a keypad and this opened the steel cage in which he was now standing. Dragon-mouthed stalactites dripped a phosphoric welcome. A maze of gantries and hydraulic supports added an industrial grandeur. There were side-rooms and living rooms, work rooms and rest rooms and, in the main chamber, resting on a steel track raised seven feet above the cavern floor, was the pearl-white spaceship itself. The door was open. Charlie shouted a greeting.

"Good morning, Charlie," said Steve emerging from inside. "Did you manage to sleep last night?"

Charlie said 'Yes' whilst frowning at what Steve was wearing, a red leather jumpsuit.

"Do you like it?" asked Steve.

"No," said Charlie.

"I thought it would add a bit of showbiz panache?"

Charlie shook his head as he walked up the ramp and into the ship.

"The young have no imagination," said Steve to himself.

Inside the ship, Charlie held up the carrier bag.

"Packed lunch?" asked Steve. "Put it in fridge."

The fridge was exactly that, a shop-bought fridge badged with the maker's marker. Indeed, if a photographer picked the right angles, photographs taken inside the spaceship could give the impression of having been taken inside an English country house. The chairs were oak and leather. There was a bookcase and a writing desk. But, in the maze of markings on the floor, there was a hint that all of this could slide away and change into something quite different. With the food in the fridge, Charlie sat down in a leather armchair and gripped the sides. He liked the chair's solidity. It made him feel safe.

"I've re-lacquered the floor. It looks good doesn't it?"

Charlie nodded.

"The smell will go away about a week after we get back."

They both laughed. "I went for a walk, early, over to Horsepool Hill," said Steve. "There's quite a crowd there."

"Grandad took me for a look on Tuesday. There were about fifty people there then."

"There are many more than that now. I've been running tests to see if the broadcast transmitters will cause interference with our electronics. There doesn't seem to be a problem but, to make sure, I think we should take her for a quick spin instead of going straight to Horsepool Hill."

"Where to?"

"Just to the capital and back, and a long slow hover over the crowd after we've taken off, when the satellite interference will be at its peak. Should we get the show on the road?"

Charlie nodded.

Steve raised his head to the computer banks hidden in the ceiling and said: "Let's go." The door closed. Charlie and Steve exchanged smiles. To the sounds of rock rolling on rock, the cavern wall opened. The track carrying the spaceship extended outwards until the spaceship was in daylight, ringed by a horseshoe of high trees, with a full sky above.

"To London, please," said Steve. "Looping low round Big Ben, and avoiding all known air routes and pigeons."

"Just pigeons?" asked Charlie.

"All birds and bees and living things. And get us back to Horsepool Hill for the set time."

The spaceship did exactly that; transporting man and boy East and West across England and making the day of everyone who saw it. Film of the spaceship had been playing daily and nightly on most broadband and television channels. The country already had their eyes to the sky.

"It's quite big London, isn't it?" said Charlie, as they eased through London airspace. This was the first time he had been to the capital city.

"Yes," said Steve. "But this isn't the first time you've been to London. You came here when you were very small. That's Big Ben up ahead."

"Big Ben's Victorian, isn't it?"

"It is," said Steve. "And, as you can see, it's really quite splendid."

Chapter 6

On Horsepool Hill, on instructions from Grandad, who was well-known in the area, the police had cleared and cordoned a landing spot sixty metres across. When the spaceship landed, the crowd around the perimeter was twenty deep. There were gasps, applause, shrieks of genuine astonishment, and a surprising amount of tears. Steve frowned at the sight of a grown man crying.

"What are you frowning about?" asked Charlie.

"I really must try to be a more modest man."

"What do you mean?"

"I'm surprised to find myself surprised at making elementary mistakes."

"You're still not making sense," said Charlie.

"Last week, I'd forgotten to prime the press and nobody came. This week, the press and the public are here, but if we step outside we'll be blinded by camera phones. Look."

Outside, a daylight firework show fired from five thousand automatic flashlights prompted into life by the low gray light of an English summer. "All popping like a chain-reaction in a nuclear bubble-wrap factory."

"There's no such thing as a nuclear bubble-wrap factory," said Charlie.

"I was being poetic. It's not a good sign to be faced with a problem I hadn't anticipated before we get going."

"We'll be all right," said Charlie, brightly. "We'll be *fine*."

Steve asked if Charlie had brought sunglasses.

"What for?"

From a cupboard drawer, Steve took out two identical pairs. He gave one to Charlie, "Be careful with them. They're from Graceland." He told Charlie to try them on. They were too big for the boy.

"Do I look like The King?"

"You look fine," said Steve. "We only need to wear them until the crowd stops flash-gunning us. Are you ready?"

"Yes," said Charlie.

"Door open." The door opened.

"Stay close." The ramp descended. Steve and Charlie stepped out into a gasping crowd that motioned like the sea. The police cordon held. Frightened by the surge of the crowd, Charlie reached for Steve's hand but Steve had raised it as a sign that he wanted to speak. They had joked about saying 'Klattu barada nikto', from the spaceman in the film *The Day The Earth Stood Still,* but the earnest emotion of the crowd meant that an in-joke wouldn't feel right. When Steve spoke, silence spread outwards in a concentric circle like a pebble thrown into a pond.

"We're sorry about the sunglasses but your flashbulbs gave us no choice. If you switch them off, and I do mean off, there is quite enough light to take a photograph without using a flash, then we'll take off the glasses and answer your questions."

A shockwave of camera flashes and phone flashes fired after Charlie and Steve took off their sunglasses.

"Yes, our names are Steve Atherton and Charlie Ellis."

"We're both English."

"I'm one sixth Polish."

"I can't remember not knowing him. He lives near me."

"No, my parents were Vivian and Randolph Ellis. They died in a car crash on the Stroud Road."

"No, I don't."

"Charlie designed the spaceship."

"From the one in *The Day The Earth Stood Still.* I have it on disc. Grandad's got it on film. Yes, real film."

"It's mostly a titanium alloy with a graphite lining."

"No, because the scientific community is much too much in the pocket of the military."

"Because the military too often does wrong even when it is doing right."

"I don't know how fast it can go. I haven't done the maths."

"From the sun."

"Yes, I am *the* Steve Atherton who made a 'fortune' in the aerospace industry."

"Yes, there is another sponsor but they will not be named."

"I'm sorry. I can't answer that question."

"Charlie *can* answer that one."

"We're going to Mars. A D.T.T.M. A Day Trip to Mars. We're going to land on Mars and walk on Mars in forty-eight hours time."

"Turn your telescopes to Mars and you'll see us there. There'll also be a more or less unbroken transmission, from the moment we take off, available to the channels that have paid the subscription fee. Thirty-three channels signed up but only the twenty-two who paid will receive it."

"No, like it says in the contracts, we'll have the sound turned off for our own security. But we'll make at least one audio-visual broadcast from the surface of the planet."

"We aim to plant the Union Jack on every planet in the solar system."

"Each planet has its own problems but nothing is insurmountable."

"Because nothing is insurmountable."

The press conference was terminated, and the mission started, after a suitably dramatic pause caused by a policeman, Officer Adams, touching the spaceship and being knocked out, his hair briefly aflame. "He'll be okay if he doesn't have a heart problem," said Steve standing up after examining the stricken man. "He'll come round in a few minutes but he'll be sore for a week. Sorry about that. But adults really should know not to touch what isn't theirs."

As silently as it had landed, the spaceship rose vertically into the lowering sky and hovered sixty feet above the applauding phone flashes and camera lights. Like a pearl-dressed diva, it bowed this way and that as Steve ran tests. There were gasps and screams from the crowd.

"What a silly question about, Do I have any *pets*?", said Charlie, an indignant frown darkening his brow.

"Don't let that upset you. Adults who know nothing about children can only condescend them. The sad thing is, she's probably got children of her own, and treats them with such mindless condescension that they'll come to mirror her own mediocrity."

"What do you mean?"

"If someone is talked down to from birth, then day by day their mind closes in on itself to protect itself. People become the role they're shaped into. It's human nature. It's a way of staying sane. But pets are good. They teach one about love and responsibility."

"Have you ever had a pet?"

"No... Well, there's no interference from the transmitters. And the outside broadcast has begun. Do you want to do the honours?"

Charlie stood up, almost shoulder to shoulder with Steve and, in a slightly heightened voice, full of the pomp of youth, he said: "Take us to Mars. We want to be parked safely within her orbit in forty-five hours time." But nothing happened. Charlie's posture dropped a little. "What did I forget?"

"The ignition code."

"Oh, yes. *Please.*"

Steve smiled. There was the briefest and sweetest wind-whistle as the spaceship rose vertically like a high-speed elevator until it broke clear of the Earth's orbit. In the vacuum of star-dotted blackness, the ship circled outwards at a banked angle for five seconds, before breaking out of the curved trajectory at a speed beyond the imagination of all but the very wise and the very young.

"It's time for the song," said Steve. They had made it a point to start their every mission with the playing of their favourite song.

"Lights!" said Charlie. The lights dimmed inside the cabin to bring the stars outside into clearer view.

"And... music!" said Steve. The music played all around them, a recording of Elvis Presley singing of the origins of the Universe and telling of the miracle of Everlasting Life.

Chapter 7

"Hi, Grandma. Hi, Grandad. This is Charlie. Hopefully, by now, you'll be getting the continuous pictures. You don't have to watch all of it. Just tune in whenever you like. All is well, as you can see, but I thought you'd like this face-to-face thing because it's more

like a letter, and there is only you getting it. Steve hasn't been able to pick up the radio signals he knows are being broadcast from Earth because, well, he'll be embarrassed by me telling you this, but he forgot to re-install the receiver after making some adjustments to it last week. He says it's on the table by the teapot in his office, and you can hit it with a hammer for him. But everything else is working well. These pictures are about three or four minutes old, so I would have grown a bit from the time you're actually watching them. And I would have combed my hair and things. We'll be entering Mars's orbit in about an hour. What?
Sorry, Steve says we'll be there in twenty minutes. So that's good. Then we'll spend about three hours orbiting the planet, taking photographs, and choosing a landing spot.
I slept well last night but I didn't go to bed until one o'clock in the morning, which you probably know already.

What? Steve says the time on the screen is wrong and I went to bed at ten o'clock; but it's not really wrong. I just wasn't tired. There was so much to do. I read three chapters of the Ernest Hemingway book you gave me, Grandad. It's very good, of course, and I know it's important to learn about other cultures and to not be judgemental, but I don't like bullfighting. I'll read it through though.

I hope all is well back home, and that the newspaper and television people have gone, and are not still taking over the café and the shop. Oh, erm, thank you Grandma for the sandwiches and the cake. Steve sends his thanks for his piece. He says it was delicious. For dinner, last night, we had roast beef and boiled potatoes and carrots, the fresh ones you'd topped and tailed, not the frozen ones. Well, that's all for now. I can see from the monitor at the side of this camera that Mars has come into clear view. It really is red. It's great. I'm going to end this broadcast by switching to an outside camera so you can see what I'm seeing. You can pretend it's the picture on the front of a postcard.

With all my love,

Charlie."

Chapter 8

A Martian summer lasts twice as long as a good summer in England but that doesn't mean there is twice as much chance of arriving on a good day. On a planet without surface water, dust is king. And dust likes to travel. In springtime on Mars, when the polar wastelands of frozen carbon dioxide start to melt, and the rising temperatures wake the winds from their winter slumber, the cold goes where it's hot, and the hot goes where it's cold, dancing dust into storms so fierce they engulf the entire planet. But this was midsummer. In the North East, a single dust storm wriggled out towards the equator. From outer space it looked like a giant worm.

"It doesn't look like it's moving at all," said Charlie.

"Look at the tip," said Steve."Oh, yes."

"And look at the sides."

"Wow!"

"Have you read *Dune*?" asked Steve.

"Some of it. I preferred the film."

"Ah, speaking of film, let me show you how to use the outside cameras again. I've made some adjustments since you last had a go." Steve pressed buttons on a wall panel. Things moved. "Take a seat."

Charlie sat down.

"Until you've mastered the camera, start with the setting at 50mm because that's the view closest to the human eye, so it will be the most faithful record, from a human perspective, of what you're looking at. Then feel free to use the whole scale. And remember to balance the composition. The subject doesn't have to be in the middle of the picture, the use of empty space is an important part of photography. And don't neglect the corners of the frame. The zoom is pretty good. If you push it towards its limits, like this, the image breaks up in the viewfinder. See? It becomes pixilated, that's a problem with digital photography. It can be reconfigured later but it makes it impossible to judge texture. When you get bored taking photographs we'll choose a landing spot."

"I'm bored already," said Charlie, flashing an 'only joking' grin.

Steve briefly switched the ship's controls to manual and took the spaceship in closer. They were briefly shaken by the wind.

"Are the images you're getting sharp?"

"I don't know," said Charlie.

"They're stored here," explained Steve, back at Charlie's side, pressing buttons that released folders of captured light. "You look at them by doing this, and this."

"Oh, yes. I remember now."

The images shuffled and grew in size according to commands issued by movements of Steve's hands and fingers. "To maintain sharpness you have to make sure that the shutter speed and the transit speed are matched. These numbers here tell you that they are."

"How?"

"The last three digits are the same. I'll keep the speed of the ship constant to make it easier for you. Nod when you've nailed it."

Charlie took photographs of the storm and nodded when he'd nailed it.

"Yes. They're great," said Steve. "They're very good indeed. Let's move on." He took the spaceship away from the storm and flew southwards to a place that looked "like Monument Valley at sunset".

"What's Monument Valley?"

"A place used in westerns by John Ford."

"Who's John Ford?"

"He made westerns starring John Wayne. Poetic films about the brotherhood of man."

"Have I seen any?"

"Some. *The Horse Soldiers*."

"*A Fistful of Dynamite*? I like *A Fistful of Dynamite*."

"That's Sergio Leone. There is no brotherhood in Leone."

Flying West, they broke from daylight into darkness and, in the darkness, they cut a repeating figure of eight between the two Martian moons, Phobos and Deimos, whose names mean Panic and Terror. They were quite a sight.

"Ship slow," said Steve. "Ceiling screens open."

The internal ceiling slid away to give an unbroken view of the night sky. Charlie Ellis gasped. An unexplored planet rolled beneath them. The moon, Phobos, passed overhead, pock-marked with impact craters. It looked impressively tough, like the face of an old battered boxer.

"Data Control Desk," said Steve. Three banks of three-tiered keyboards rose from within the floor. Above the keyboards, a single semi-transparent semi-circular screen opened and stretched to its full length. "Screen on," said Steve. The screen glowed into life. "And take us higher." Like an electronic musician in concert, Steve spent a busy hour tapping keyboards to send out requests which brought back information. He kept his attention on the screen as they lapped the planet seven times along seven different compass points.

Charlie noticed that sweat was collecting on Steve's brow. "Heating down," softly said the boy.

"We're enormously lucky to find the planet so welcoming," announced Steve with an air of surprise. "There are strong winds here and there but nothing that will give us trouble. I was going to break for lunch, but let's land while the conditions are good. You can choose almost anywhere you want. The North East is out, of course, but you can choose anywhere else."

"So we don't have to land on the Earth side of Mars?" On the side that would be visible to telescope users on Earth.

"That would be useful, I suppose, and we must do at least one landing there, but you can choose wherever you want."

"Olympus Mons," said Charlie, not missing a beat.

"I knew you'd say that."

Boys who know about Mars will choose Olympus Mons because, at twenty miles high, it is not only the biggest volcano on Mars, it's the biggest volcano in the solar system. Boys take pleasure in looking at things that are big. To the ship's computer, Steve said: "Olympus Mons. Fix a position when we are over the summit."

Charlie remembered the time back on Earth when Steve had used porridge and a series of plastic bowls punched with holes to explain to Charlie's grandparents why Martian volcanoes were so big. "Mars formed at the same time as the Earth, but it's smaller than the Earth so it cooled more quickly and more compactly when it formed, so the Martian crust doesn't move. The Earth's crust is always moving. There are always eruptions from the Earth's core. Magma, molten rock, leaks through in various places, like this." He forced a fistful of porridge through holes in a bowl to make a series of porridge mountains. "But because the Martian crust was solid and still, the lava piled up in the same place. See. See the difference? On Mars, that place is called Olympus Mons."

Steve was trying and failing to enthuse Grandma about the Day Trip To Mars. She hadn't been impressed by photographs of the volcano. She thought it looked like a teenage pimple. "A pimple that has been allowed to go septic."

"That's because you don't understand the concept of scale," said Steve. "This volcano is massive. Huge. That hugeness can't be conveyed by a photograph."

Grandma, who extended a benevolent maternal severity to all males she thought worth bothering about, knew the psychology behind any man's action, and stopped listening after the words *you don't understand.* She waited patiently for Steve Atherton to finish what he was saying and what he was doing. Then after a suitable pause, which attracted everyone's attention to her, she said, "All I can see is you wasting good food because you don't like the doctor telling you to eat porridge to lower your cholesterol."

Steve blushed. Charlie grinned and Grandad erupted with laughter, pleased that The Truth had been dealt to someone other than himself.

The spaceship was hovering over the crater of Olympus Mons. In a little less than five minutes time, the pictures would be received by broadcasting stations and research institutes on Earth, where they would be greeted by awe and astonishment. One fifth of the world's population was watching. Fortunately for our adventurers, but to the chagrin of readers hoping for descriptions of red bubbling lava, there hasn't been a volcanic eruption on Mars for forty nine million, three hundred and fourteen years, when Mars had an almost Earth-like weather system.

The sight soon to be astonishing viewers back home was the hitherto unimaginable glory of the cliffs that ringed the rim of the volcano. They were six kilometres high and sheer. Steve shook his head: "Can you imagine the greatness of the person who started at Mars ground zero and who conquered that cliff?"

"It's not a very steep volcano, with the exception of those cliffs," said Charlie.

"And the enscarpment at the base. And the Calderas. They're impossibly steep in parts. That cliff is higher than Everest."

"You can tell you want to climb it," said Charlie.

"Climb it? I haven't the skills."

Charlie smiled.

"And I haven't the equipment, and we haven't the time."

Charlie's smile widened.

"Stop trying to egg me on." After a pause, during which Charlie did nothing but smile at him, Steve said: "Did you do any climbing when you were in the scouts?"

"I'm still in the scouts," said Charlie. "I climbed Snowdon last year."

"That's not climbing, it's walking."

"It's steeper than most of Mons and the gravity on Earth is much higher."

"Did you enjoy it?"

"Not really. The weather wasn't good so there wasn't a view. In fact you couldn't see more than twenty metres in front of you. But I was glad there was a toilet on top."

"A toilet?"

"On the top, and a café and a shop. We left so early in the morning there wasn't time for me to go to the toilet. I was desperate by the time we reached the top."

"Well, crapping on Mars is out of the question. It's too cold. Your bum would freeze off. I think we should land in the crater of Mons, with those cliffs as our backdrop. I can run some tests to make sure we are out of range of rockfall. Then we can do another landing on the plain for the telescopes watching from Earth. Roll with the sun, so to speak. There are probably four hours of good light here until the night starts closing in. It's going to be a good day, Charlie Ellis. Are you ready to land?"

Charlie nodded. He stood up. Back straight. Shoulders back. To the ship's computer he said: "Hologram. Mars."

A hologram glowed forth showing the planet of Mars. "Olympus Mons." The hologram zoomed in to the volcano. "Zoom in closer... South of the collapse crater in the North West corner... The rounder one. Yes, that looks like a good spot. Inspection, please." Then to Steve, he said: "What you grinning at?"

"Nothing. You're doing great."

Strings of strong yellow light shone out from beneath the spaceship and inspected the landing area almost like fingers. The inspection took only a few seconds. The lights withdrew one by one. When the last of them was extinguished, a blue beam burst forth and locked onto the point of ground selected as the landing spot. Steve read the information coming back into the computers.

"It's kick-dusty but stable. There's a five-to-ten percent chance we'll step into dust right up to our middle. But let's give it a go. Take her down."

Charlie said: "Spaceship. Land on Mars... please."

The spaceship decended vertically to the surface of Mars. As it descended, small steel legs shaped like bird-claws emerged from the underside of the ship and, with a comedy which suggested they were almost human, the legs rearranged themselves to counter a slight incline on the floor of the crater. The landing was safe and comfortable.

"We're there," said Steve. "We're on Mars."

"Thank you."

Charlie offered him his hand. They shook hands.

"Let's get ready to go out."

Chapter 9

In the year before making the journey to Mars, Steve, Charlie and Grandma spent six weekends designing the spacesuits. Their aim was to add a bit of style and colour to a range more noted for bulk than appearance. "Remember from your lesson last week," said Grandma, "that Britain was once the fashion capital of the world."

"Twiggy," said Charlie.

"Yes," said Grandma, "but Twiggy modelled clothes. She didn't design them, as far as I know. What did we decide were the Four Great Laws of Fashion?"

"The Style, the Quality of the cloth or material," said Steve.

"The Practicality and the Purpose," said Charlie.

"Yes, there's no style without purpose. It's all for one and none without four. Which means?"

"That we have to have a silver spacesuit," said Steve.

Charlie had wanted a red one in honour of his favourite football team, but the heat-shielding and heat-preserving qualities of silver were proving too practical an advantage to ignore.

"I think so," said Gran, "but the wool lining can be any colour you want it to be."

"We could add a red trim to the cuffs," said Charlie, "and pretend it's the away kit?"

Months of testing brought the suits ever closer to the cumbersome designs favoured by Astronauts and Cosmonauts, but there were innovations. Like the spaceship itself, the suits drew energy from the sun and used it to regulate the temperature inside the suit. Solar energy also powered button-sized cameras in the shoulders. The camera on the right shoulder recorded what was in front of the wearer. The camera on the left recorded what was behind. Splendidly low-tech microphones allowed verbal communication. Charlie's spacesuit also carried an embroided patch he'd designed for his logo - two Gunwald swords on a red and white background. The boots were built by a firm in Northampton, with later adjustments by Steve to allow them to respond to changes in gravity.

Steve and Charlie suited up and entered the airlock, a small room revealed when a wall panel opened and which closed behind them when they were inside it. Steve checked the seal of the inner door. On the wall to the left of the airlock's outer door were nine small British flags, cotton on spiked stainless steel poles. Above each flag was written the name of a planet. To the right of the flags were the helmets. They secured and checked their helmets.

Now, standing shoulder to shoulder, Steve pressed buttons on the wall that removed the room's oxygen. When that was complete, he told Charlie to stand back, and he pressed the button which opened the outer door and released a short landing ramp. There was a whistle-howl of wind. From inside the spaceship they could only see a wall of rock to the East of them. Charlie took a deep breath and was about to step outside when Steve Atherton stopped him. A hand on Charlie's arm. "Don't go out."

"What's wrong?"

"Turn off the cameras," said Steve.

"What?"

"Please turn off your cameras, Charlie."

Charlie did as he was told. Steve closed the outer door. It closed with a satisfyingly safe completeness, a rim coming from within the door itself to fuse it with the wall that framed it. "This is too important a moment to share with the world. You're about to become the first person ever to walk on a planet that isn't Earth. The film of you walking on Mars, for the first time, will be played and replayed until the public think it and you are theirs." Charlie didn't quite understand what Steve meant, but the words chimed with what Grandad had said to him. In the main room of the spaceship, Steve turned off all the external cameras, an act which gave conspiracy theorists years of conjecture, and said: "We'll go for a walk on our own first. Then we'll come back and do it again for the people watching back home. Are you ready to go?"

Charlie nodded. Before stepping out, he motioned a kiss to the red trim of his cuffs.

"Door open."

Charlie walked out and took a dozen kick-dusty steps. Then he looked up and up and up and up. He looked so high, up looking for the top of the cliffs, an impossible towered wall of red rock, that he almost fell over. He was not normally excited by geographical features, but he had to sit down to stop his head from spinning. He would have almost certainly wept had Steve not tapped him on the shoulder and said: "It's not bad is it?"

There was no verbal response from the boy.

"Come on, Charlie. Let's get back to the ship, and do one for the cameras. Have you thought of something to say when you take the first steps?"

"What?"

"One small step for mankind, that sort of thing. It's the job of the artist to help the media to tell the story."

"What?" said Charlie, still a little disorientated, but his emotions now returning to his full control.

"The first words are important, Charlie. Remember, we'll be broadcasting sound as well as pictures."

"*Are* the first words really important, Steve?"

"They are if you say the right ones. You've had months to think of something.""I have been thinking about it," said Charlie earnestly, "trying to think of something to say, but I haven't really come up with anything yet. Do you have any ideas?"

They were almost back at the spaceship.

"No, the words must be your own, Charlie. The only advice I would want to give is they shouldn't be sentimental."

"Why not?"

"Sentimentality is emotion that hasn't been earned. So it lacks truth."

Charlie pondered this for a moment before asking: "What would Elvis say?"

"Elvis was an artist and a Christian. He would praise God sincerely and be humble and graceful. But you're not Elvis Presley. You're Charlie Ellis."

"What would you say?"

"I'm an engineer. I'd talk about advancing engineering and science by feeding them with the lost arts of imagination and ambition, as a way to realise man's potential, but they are not phrases I've heard you say, and they are not words that come honestly from a teenager's mouth. You're on your own, Charlie. You're the first Anglonaut." *Anglonaut* was a word Charlie had invented in his infancy when reading about Astronauts and Cosmonauts and wondering what an English space explorer would be called.

He never did think of anything suitably profound or quotable to accompany the first filmed footsteps on the surface of Mars, though the words he came up with had a certain unintended prophecy. After stepping out onto and into the vermilion dust, he walked forward ten steps; looked back at Steve, standing in the doorway of the airlock, and he said: "Steve, can you hear me?"

They took photographs, collected dust and rock samples and, mostly in silence and without ceremony, they planted the flag.

"How long do you think it'll last?" asked Charlie.

"It'll stay there until someone steals it. Did you take a good picture?"

"I think so," said Charlie, a reply which always gets the response to take another. Steve smiled. Charlie pressed the button.

"Should I take one last one of you?" asked Steve.

"If you want to."

Charlie gave the camera to Steve and struck a suitable pose. By luck, the sun was in the right place to give the photograph a deserving spectacle. Thus was taken the image for the biggest selling poster of the year. More than three million copies were sold in the first months it went on sale.

Now, with the outer door of the spaceship closed, Steve and Charlie walked the half-mile to the edge of the collapse creator, a circular bowl two thousand feet deep.

"It's incredible, isn't it?" said Steve. "Absolutely extraordinary."

Charlie could only nod in response. He was surprised and confused by the emotions building inside of him. He had always been the very model of a level-headed boy. He had never before been quick to emotion.

Chapter 10

The second landing on Mars, the first recorded by telescopes and cameras on Earth, took place five-and-a-half hours later, after a long lunch lengthened by Steve because he could see that Charlie was over-exhilarated and edging towards exhaustion. He knew that the boy's emotions had to be brought down, his heartbeat returned to an easier rhythm, for the safety of the mission, because a hot head burns commonsense. In those moments of Charlie's near exhilaration, Steve Atherton had his first regret about bringing the boy along. Something had changed inside Charlie. Steve had not anticipated that that would be the case. The unimagined spectacle and the slow-dawning awareness of a sense of their achievements had awakened a new consciousness in Charlie that was as frightening to the boy as it was exhilarating. Aware of the fragility of new-born things, Steve gave Charlie room enough and time enough to tire himself out and calm himself down. He eased the boy's attention on to safer things by directing it to the dust, the soil and the rock samples, the bagging, the labelling, the storing, and: "Do you think we should rest a while? Take a nap and do the filmed recording in the morning?"

"No," said Charlie. "I'm okay. I want to go back out."

Having thus drawn a line under Landing One, with all things signed and sealed, Steve told Charlie to "put your happy face back on because we'll be talking to the good folks at Jordrell Bank."

Charlie nodded.

"Where do you want to land?"

"You can choose this time," said Charlie.

Steve brought the ship down near the planet's equator, on the Elysium Planitia, where they picked a carrier bag full of small rocks and took some very good photographs. They both said *Hello* to Earth, and they opened up the sound channels for a twenty-three minute walk and talk that they broadcast live from the Martian surface. Steve brought the broadcast to a close when he noticed condensation was forming inside his helmet. He said: "I don't think it will be a problem, but electronics and water don't mix, and there's no point in pushing the risk. Let's get back inside."

Later in the day, they took the ship northward again and brought it down in sight of two dust devils - two spinning columns of dust. There is film of the two devils spinning in astonishingly close proximity, but that footage was taken from a wide-angled lens and did not conform to the view from the human eye.

"How would you stop them?"

"Those? A stick of dynamite would stop those. The explosion would break the weight and directions of the wind, but why would you want to? In general, dust devils stop themselves by becoming too greedy. They pick up so much dust that they become too heavy to move quickly. When they slow down, the wind speed drops, and the dust falls to the ground. That's a lesson all of us could learn."

"Why are they called devils? Is it because of the redness?"

"Possibly, but if you look closely at the head of the spinning column you can see the Devil's face. Look, I can see it quite clearly."

"No, you can't," said Charlie.

"Yes, I can. Look. Eyes. Nose. Ears. Cloak." He pointed to the head of the storm.

"You're just trying to scare me," said Charlie. "There's nothing there but dust."

"And from what is mankind made?" asked Steve.

"From dust," said Charlie.

"It is dust from which we are born. And it is to dust that we return. And there is a face in that storm, Charlie. There are many faces. I can see the living faces of men and women waiting to be born here."

Chapter 11

When they returned to the airlock for the last time that day, stamping their boots on the floor to get the dust off, and changing out of their suits, they both suddenly felt very tired. Looking at his watch, still set to British Summer Time, Steve calculated that they had been up and active for almost twenty-four hours. "History has been made today, Charlie, but we'll both be ill if we don't eat and drink something nutritious and if we don't get some sleep. What have you eaten today?"

"Just a chocolate bar and some swig since lunch."

"I'll have the pork chops and potatoes ready in about half-an-hour. I don't want you going to sleep until you've eaten. Do you think you can stay awake until then?"

"Yes," said Charlie, "but I'm too tired to write my journal."

"Get some swig and a snack from the fridge, and it would be good if you could send a message back to your grandparents."

"Okay," said Charlie. He sent Grandma a short smile-happy message, a sparkle in his eyes betraying his fatigue, then, as the spaceship filled with the smell of home cooking, he sorted out his collection of Martian rocks, arranging them on the kitchen table in ascending order of size. With a press-seal plastic bag, he returned to the airlock and scooped another good sample of Martian dust from the mats on the floor. He held it up to the light. He had intended the collection to be a gift for the space research centre in Leicester, but tiredness brought on a sentimental phase and he was having second thoughts. He wanted to keep it all for himself.

Back on Earth, film of the first (second) walk on Mars was playing in looped repetition on ninety-four television stations, and on an almost uncountable number of internet channels, most of the official subscribers having sub-leased the footage to their competitors. Fourteen cameras had each recorded more than ten hours of Steve and Charlie on Mars. The more established television channels, with the exception of the BBC who had not paid the subscription fee, were hard at work editing the material into show-case programmes they hoped would win awards. But, in the coming years, the unedited footage, broadcast in its entirety only on a regional German channel, proved to be the most prized and the most commercially successful. People all around the world bought copies of the unedited film to use as the backdrop to their own Martian dreams. Under license, the Disney corporation used the

German footage to build the century's most popular theme park ride, The Martian Adventure, complete with a gravity-reduction chamber, towered walls of red rock, and a dust devil.

But Charlie and Steve never made it to Disneyland.

"Beds out," said Steve, after clearing away the dishes. From the floor at opposite sides of the room emerged two duvet covered beds. "It's been a good day," said Charlie, undressing.

"It's been great," agreed Steve. "The ship is programmed to get us home in, well, thirty-one hours or so but, if you don't mind, I'd like to stop the ship in six hours time so we can do a bit of stargazing. At that point, the sun will be giving us perfect views of Venus and Mercury. We haven't had the chance yet to really test the telescopes."

"Sounds good," said Charlie.

"And if we spend the afternoon stargazing, we can have another short nap and arrive back at Horsepool Hill in daylight."

"And I can polish up my journal for Grandad."

"We'll do that then," said Steve.

The computer was stubborn at first when Steve tried to pro-gramme in the new instructions but, after a bit of forcing, it did as it was told. It stopped the flight back to Earth at 06.22 GMT. So the spaceship never made it back to Earth.

Chapter 12

Charlie had difficulty sleeping. And the sleep that came was troubled with dreams. In his dream, he was shown and re-shown his parents' death. They were driving back from somewhere. Charlie couldn't remember where. Was it an airshow? or was it a rugby match? He had no memory of the day other than what was shown in the dream. He was on the back seat of a car. He remem-bered having difficulty with his seatbelt. He locked the belt first into the wrong receiver, then he unlocked it and fastened it into the right one. He could feel the shiny metal in his hands. The road ahead was busy and narrow and everyone was driving too fast. He remembered looking over his father's shoulder at the speedometer and noting it was above the legal limit. But he didn't say anything because he knew that to do so would turn his father's temper. There were lorries on the road. And there was a van. A white van.

"Oh, what is he doing?" said Charlie's father.

Then Charlie's father and mother were dead. And Charlie slept for a long time. In his sleep, he sometimes heard voices, and sometimes he saw faces of people he didn't know. He remembered seeing his Grandmother's face. She said: "I think he's trying to speak. Jim. Get the doctor."

This dream of death came in the last moments of the spaceship's existence. A collision threw Charlie and Steve out of their beds. The lights came on, flickered and faltered and failed.

Steve shouted: "Into the shuttle!"

Charlie stamped on a panel in the floor which opened to reveal two sub-level seats. He jumped into one of the seats and fastened the shoulder straps and seat belt. Across the room, at the control panel, Steve pressed buttons which released a disc, smaller and much thicker than a CD. With the disc in his hand, he ran across the room to join Charlie.

"Shuttle away." In an instant, the seats on which they were sitting were roofed, and the shuttle was falling away from the prone spaceship. Looking upwards, Charlie and Steve could see the spaceship tilting and spinning as if in mockery of the take-off dance it performed for the crowd on Horsepool Hill. Then the spaceship exploded in a wince-making burst of racing white light. The shuttle shook violently as it top-tailed in decreasingly fast circles, head over heels, over heels, over heels, until it was level again and back under Steve's control. He turned off the engines and asked Charlie was he all right?

There was a smear of blood on Charlie's face, wiped there by his hand after he had felt for and found a wound on his shin. "I banged it when I jumped in. It doesn't hurt." The wound was already matting, darkening, two lighter streaks of blood raced down the sides of his leg. "It looks worse than it is," said Charlie.

"Put your palm over the wound and press down. Support it with your other hand."

Charlie did as he was told and asked: "What happened, Steve?"

Steve put the disc into the control panel: "We must have hit something. We'll find out in a minute. A meteorite or some space junk." He typed as he talked. "I saw a crack spreading across the hull of the ship."

A shiver ran from Charlie's backbone to his temples and down to his stomach. He thought he was going to be sick. He whispered: "Are we safe?"

"We're still breathing," was Steve's answer. He knew in an instant that that wasn't good enough. "Yes, we're safe." The screen in front of Steve was a maze of lines and numbers all changing and dancing to the clicking rhythm played by his fingers. Then a film played. Then six films were playing on the one screen. Steve switched between the films, making one bigger, then reducing it and bringing up another until it took up most of the screen. Then he settled on one film and said: "My God!"

A coal black meteorite, huge and with a jagged edge, hit the spaceship full on. It paused, briefly, as if to marvel at the damage it had done. Then, like a whale beneath a rowing boat, it rolled away into the blackness. The picture on the screen stayed for less than a minute more.

"Why did the spaceship explode?" asked Charlie. "We weren't carrying fossil fuel?"

"We were carrying liquid oxygen, unavoidably. Unstable." Steve continued to type. His eyes fixed on the screen. "It shouldn't have happened. I'd checked the flight path and it was clear. And, in any-case, the radar should have picked up a rock of that size. Oh dear, this number here means that the data on the disc is from the back-up computer, which means that the main computer was down."

"You did tell it to turn itself off," said Charlie.

"Did I?"

"I think so. You said something about *stop* at six o'clock."

"And it took me at my word. But why wasn't the back-up computer working?"

"It was recording," said Charlie.

"It was recording data, yes, but it wasn't doing anything else. It wasn't performing any of the life support or security duties."

"Was it programmed to?"

"Yes, but something went wrong. Nothing was working. Nothing at all. For almost four hours there had been no oxygen circulating. We were dying in our sleep."

Charlie's temples tingled. "Then the meteorite saved us. The meteorite woke us up?"

"Well, we're awake. And there are problems to overcome. But I'll get you home."

"What problems?"

"We're eighteen million miles from Earth. The shuttle is a docking and landing vehicle, not a transport craft. Its top speed is less than six thousand miles an hour."

"But it can get us back, can't it?"

Steve continued to tap keys. "Your maths is as good as mine, Charlie."

Charlie did the calculations and said: "Did you say it travels at exactly six thousand miles an hour?"

"Five thousand eight hundred."

"Then ... we'll be home in... or at least in Earth's orbit in... three thousand, one hundred and one or two hours, give or take."

"Yes, or one-hundred-and-twenty-nine days."

"Well, I can put up with you for that long."

"Thank you," said Steve. "The navigation unit and the compass have been damaged by the shock waves from the explosion. Until I can get an accurate fix we'll have to fly by sight. Point ourselves in the right direction. But which direction? A tiny miss means a long long way off course. Can you see the Earth? It's a pale blue dot."

They looked all around. They looked and they looked but they could not see the Earth. And they could not see Mars. They could see stars and they could see the sun. Then they were showered with debris from the explosion, which included a photograph of Charlie Ellis's grandparents.

"Radio our position," said Charlie.

"A transmitter is easy enough to make but it would probably mean dismantling something that's already working. I'll need to do an inventory before we can do that. I think if we simply sit tight, the Earth will eventually show itself. It's probably on the far side of the sun. It'll come into view each day, if we're looking for it in the right place at the right time. Remind me to put a pair of binoculars into the shuttlecraft when we make another spaceship. Is your leg still bleeding?"

Charlie moved his hands away. "No, it's stopped."

"Good. Put a plaster on it. The first aid box is in the top drawer on the left. Then get into your suit and try to get some sleep. We'll sit tight until the Earth shows itself. Then we'll fire up the engines and go home. I'll get you home. Safely. I promise."

Chapter 13

Charlie woke to the smells of a good breakfast, hot, full, and much enjoyed, accompanied by smiles all around and an air of calmness and confidence from Steve, who had stayed up all night to do whatever he could do to ensure that the first full day inside the shuttlecraft was as stress-free for Charlie as it was possible to be. He hadn't liked seeing the look of concern on the boy's face when he had asked, "Are we safe?" He knew that to reduce the risk of psychological damage he had to manage the risks, and the boy's awareness of the risks and dangers, in such as a way as to mitigate their impact.

The day before had been one of unforseen stresses, the subduing effect of the 'mind-blowing' spectacle of the Martian sites, the adolescent jargon having an unexpected descriptive accuracy, followed by the boy's dawning awareness of their sense of special achievement, then trumped by the horror and the close-to-death experience of the exploding spaceship, the fragility of the damaged shuttlecraft, and their own imperiled position, meant that Steve knew he had try to let those internal wounds heal sufficiently before fresh wounds could be struck. And there were going to be fresh wounds. There wasn't food enough to get both of them home. Before Charlie had woken, Steve had done an inventory of the supplies and found that Providence hadn't improved them. They were exactly what they were when he, Steve Atherton, had put them there. Then his luck turned slightly, as the night turned, and a pale blue dot was lit in black space by the sun. Steve pointed the ship, fixed a position, and set the ship's engines for home.

Back on Earth, a wave of shock rolled round it and brought on full days of grief. The grieving would have gone on longer if the executives in the media had not been so quick to sign up low-looking experts ever keen to broadcast a full range of practised disapprovals. The words *foolhardy* and *innocence* were much used. The obituary writers in the national newspapers gave mostly laudatory accounts of Steve Atherton's achievements in academia and engineering, but none managed to convey the true wonder of what they presumed was a one-way Martian landing, and one used the word, *Murderer*. Many of the published accounts included a photograph of the exploding spaceship, an explosion that had been captured by two satellites and which had lowered the mood of the world.

The only person on Earth who thought that Steve and Charlie were alive was Grandma, although the initial shock had aged her a year in a day. Her husband was facing away from her in bed and deepening into a private grief when she put a hand on his shoulder and said: "He's still alive. I can feel it in my bones." Grandad hadn't talked all evening and had no intention of talking now. He had decided he wouldn't talk, and he wouldn't sleep, and he would refuse his breakfast in the morning, and he'd become ill. Then he'd take to his bed again and then he would die. So went his thoughts.

In the morning, secure in her faith that Charlie was safe, Grandma continued with her day unconcerned and uninterrupted, and this brought stares of disapproval from the proprietor of the post office, and from the rushing-pushing people from the press. *Is This The World's Most Heartless Grandmother?* ran a banner headline that failed to get the editor sacked.

Whether or not the courts would be called upon to prove the deaths of Steve Atherton and Charlie Ellis, there was already in place, under Grandad's patronage, a programme to prevent the places where Steve and Charlie had lived and worked from becoming widely known. It was known that the success of the Day Trip To Mars would bring government representatives the world over; ministers and moneymen all keen to pick the brains, and to eye the profits, of the man who, without their help, had made interplanetary travel not only possible but exclusive.

The most dangerous of these men and women, of course, were the representatives of the governments who didn't want the knowledge to fall into the wrong hands, but whose own agendas were almost exclusively militaristic. These were Steve's thoughts as he wrote a page of his Captain's Log. He knew that on returning to Earth, these war-likely fellows would approach him through all the proper and all the improper channels. He knew that on returning from Mars he would find his house to have been burgled and his computer files and research records stolen. He knew that the thefts would be made to look like they were done by a lone common thief, and that a scapegoated man would probably be found, paraded to the press (paid off) and forgotten about. And although Steve would regret the inconvenience that this would bring, he welcomed the excuse it would give him to withdraw from the public and into his own work. He knew that nothing that could be stolen from his house could bring benefit to the paymasters of the men hired to steal from him. The secrets of spaceflight were kept not on file, nor on paper, but in his head. His postgraduate introduction into the commercial world of aeronautical engineering had taught him, from hard experience, that nothing of commercial or scientific value could be kept on anything less organic than his brain. His brain's back-up was the brain of his protégé, Charlie Ellis. Charlie knew the hows and whys. Their hand-drawn designs for the spaceship, its prototypes (of which there had been three) and the blueprints for the shuttlecraft, did contain scraps of hand-scribbled maths which, if interpreted and applied correctly, could lead a scientific team to an understanding of working spaceship construction. But these plans, kept for sentimental reasons, were safe within the walls of the house of Steve Atherton's sponsor, Charlie's Grandad. The Bat Cave, of course, had secrets to yield, but its security, at least to the lone professional thief, was formidable.

Steve showed Charlie how to operate the controls of the shuttle. They were very basic. The red buttons and levers controlled things inside the ship. Blue buttons and levers operated everything on the outside of the ship. There was no voice activation unit. "That's for the window shields to open and close. We need them closed for re-entry. That's the central computer screen, on and off. Heating up. Heating down." It was all very interesting and easy.

Then Charlie asked: "Where's the toilet?"

"Do you need to go?"

"No, but I need to know where it is."

"Press the red button there and try not to scream."

Cautiously, Charlie pressed the red button and said: "*Whooah!*", as a section of the seat on which he was sitting slid away.

"It's sitting whatever the process," said Steve. The shuttle wasn't big enough to stand up in.

Charlie's first self-appointed task was to build a modesty screen using two emptied cardboard boxes which he broke up, joined together and cut out using eye-to-hand skill of impressive authority and draughtsmanship. He looked up at the curvature of the ceiling, and down at the irregular line of the floor space between their seats, then he drew and cut a perfect match-shape from the cardboard. He fastened it to the ceiling and the floor using duct tape. With the temporary modesty wall thus in place, he cut a flap into it at eye level and looked through and said: "Hello, Steve."

"If you need to have a crap just have one. I'll put some music on, and try not to breath in."

The first task Steve set Charlie was to build a transmitter and tell his grandparents he was safe. He hoped it would take Charlie a few days at least, but four hours later, Charlie had wired the box to the ship's computer and was broadcasting to the Earth. He said: "Gran, Grandad. It's Charlie. How are you? We're perfectly safe. We're a long way from home but we're coming home. It could be a while but don't worry about us. Steve's been thinking up a few plans to get us back sooner but they're still at the notebook stage. So we don't really know when we'll be home. But we're okay."

He took his finger off the button and asked Steve was that allright?

"Say something about the explosion and the shuttle so that they know you sent it after we died."

Charlie frowned at Steve in a way that said *that's not funny.* Then he pressed the transmission button and said: "The spaceship blew up but we got away in the shuttle. It's cramped but it's all right. It hit a meteorite. The spaceship that is. Or a meteorite hit us. But we're okay. I banged my leg but it's fine." He released the button. Steve nodded. He re-pressed the button and ended with, "I'll try to send another message in a few days, or when we have a proper plan. But don't worry if I don't because we need to recycle the components back into the control panel. Love to you and Grandad. Over and out, from Charlie."

Charlie handed the box back to Steve, who immediately began to dismantle it and return its components to their proper place and function.

Charlie asked: "Do you think they'll get it?"

"There's no reason why they shouldn't. It'll be the first thing they hear when they turn on the TV."

"What's for dinner?"

"What do you want?"

"A BBC," said Charlie.

"Help yourself."

A BBC was their food-speak for A Big Bag of Crisps. Like many friendships built up over years, parts of their conversation had developed a private shorthand. Theirs was most noticeable in food and in greetings. Their greetings mostly consisted of words of German origin, Heidelberg and Hindenberg, and their derivations, including Hi and Heidel and Hinden. Farewell was *Veeder*, a corruption of Auf Wiedersehn. Their food slang included a two-by-two, which meant a cooked breakfast. The breakfast could take almost any form as long as it was hot and there were two of each component: two pieces of toast, two sausages, two eggs, two rashers of bacon, two mushrooms, two spoonfuls of beans. "No, you need more beans than that. They're not part of the two-by-two," said Charlie.

Two days later, Steve Atherton prepared for the giving of the bad news by saying, "Did I ever tell you of the time when I survived two plane crashes in less than two minutes?"

"I think so," replied Charlie slowly, though he couldn't remember.

"I'd developed a new compressor engine for a new type of jet plane, independently financed in Britain, but the only folks to take it seriously were the Americans. The plane didn't have the necessary certificates for a Transatlantic flight, and the Americans sensibly wanted to keep it off the radar, and they wouldn't come to us, so we, that's Bill Butler and me - you know Bill, he works for your Grandad - Bill and I put the jet in the hold of a cargo plane, and we flew it over to a testing facility in Wyoming. The Americans took their time looking it over and rejecting all my innovations whilst logging them and using them later in their own projects. On the day we were to take the plane back to England, our carrier plane was grounded by the American inspector and, in fairness, it wasn't in the best condition when we took it across. I'd reported a couple of things that needed repairing and I'd asked for them to be repaired, but the repairs hadn't been done and other faults were found. Our generous hosts offered us a plane and a pilot to take our prototype jet back to Britain. So far, so ordinary.

We flew back at an altitude high enough to keep us off the grid. When we entered British airspace, the cargo plane went pop. It stopped working. The electrics failed. The engines failed. Everything went kaput. The American pilot, already with a parachute on his back, said it was the only one, mumbled an apology, and jumped out, never to be seen again. I looked inside the cockpit of my own plane. Our parachutes were missing. In the inquest afterwards, it emerged that the pilot was not the man the Americans claimed he was. Their pictures of their pilot didn't match the picture of the man who left us hanging there in a dead aeroplane."

"Was he a spy?"

"Who knows? He may or may not have sabotaged the plane and our parachutes. He may or may not have survived the jump. We don't know. Bill and I took stock of our options before the cargo plane stalled. We could try to pilot the cargo plane, or we could try to leave in my own plane."

"What did you do?"

"I tried a few switches and levers in the cargo plane cockpit. It wasn't a machine that I'd built. I didn't have any confidence I could get it to spark, and I couldn't get the wheels down. Nothing worked. In any case, I knew that the cockpit of my own plane would be the safest place to be when we crashed. The glass was pretty much indestructible and the roll cage was twenty times stronger than that of the cargo plane. When combined, those two factors gave us a 0.001 chance of surviving."

"You were lucky."

"Then I saw the fuel. The cargo hold was packed full of fuel, which made no sense because fuel is fuel. There was no need for the American plane to be carrying its own fuel for the return flight. And then, of course, I discovered that there was no fuel in my own plane. Well, I took a logical guess that there wouldn't be, because procedure prevented it. Then we found that the cargo doors were sealed. And there was no manual override."

"What did you do?"

"Bill's a strong guy. He picked up a tool and started punching holes in the cargo door, serating it. It was astonishing how skillfully and how quickly he worked, tearing a new door in the wall of the old one, while making sure that he didn't open up a hole big enough to pull him clean out into the sky. I set up a siphoning rig and started to get some fuel into my plane, and I released the locks that held the plane in place, and it started to roll around. Bill almost got crushed. Then things started to get really scary because the cargo plane stalled and entered its perpendicular death spin."

Charlie gasped.

"That meant we had ninety seconds to impact. Somehow or other, and it wasn't easy, Bill and I both managed to get into the cockpit of my plane and, remember, the thing is still being refuelled. The hose is still attached. And I'm flicking switches and waking the plane up. And I know that as soon as I spark the engines, the whole thing is going to go bang."

"Because of the fuel?"

"Because of the fuel."

"Why didn't you throw the fuel out?"

"Because I didn't think of that. Ideally we wanted the door of the cargo hold to open by itself, rip open from the pressure along the dotted lines made by Bill. And we hoped that we would fall away from the falling cargo plane, like we did when we escaped in the shuttle. But the serated door wouldn't go. So I fired the engines. *Bang.*"

"What happened?"

"The fuel in the cargo hold exploded, and the cargo plane exploded. We should have been blown up twice. I've no idea why we didn't explode. Perhaps I did remove the refuelling line? Except I remember leaving it in so we could take on board as much fuel as possible in as short a time as possible. Anyway, we had about twenty seconds to live. First of all, it's impossible to launch a jet plane cold in mid-air, and it's doubly difficult to launch and pilot a jet plane in turbulent air. And you just can't do it in flames. And we were falling fast. So we did the impossible."

Charlie grinned.

Steve continued: "The jet with Bill and I onboard came tumbling out of the sky, spinning so fast, and at such angles, that we seemed to go against all known laws of physics, except *one*."

"Down."

"Gravity down down down."

"Were there ejector seats?"

"Yes, but we didn't have parachutes. And we were now within about seven seconds of dying."

"Press the ejector button four seconds before impact."

"We weren't pointing in the right direction. Somehow, I must have been able to get the nose of the plane under control and I must have levelled us off because we started hitting tree tops. When we hit the second tree I knew that we would live because it meant we were flying horizontally. We had missed the ground. I remember hitting a third tree and the undercarriage collapsing. The cargo plane came down in a village called Botley, near Southampton. Guess where we landed?"

"I don't know."

"Grandad's lake. Hit the trees above it and dropped in like a stone."

"Wow!"

"Coincidence or what? Bill had whiplash and I'd pulled three discs in my spine. But we were fine. Your grandmother told me off for dripping sand and water on her carpet."

Charlie grinned. "I remember Grandad saying something about you crashing in the lake. He said (putting on a Grandad voice): "If I'd have drained the lake I wouldn't have to put up with all of this."

"All of what?"

"I don't know. Grandma was nagging him about something."

"The Americans tried to sue us for the loss of the cargo plane. They kept ours as collatoral."

"Collatoral?"

"Yes. So, you see, Master Charlie Ellis, I'm the king of crash landings. I survive them. It's what I do. So, what I'm trying to say is, don't be afraid. I'll get you home. Now, there are a few problems we need to solve."

"Problems?"

"A few things we need to overcome."

Charlie went quiet. Steve said: "We've been in the shuttle craft for three days. There are one-hundred and twenty-six more days to go. What do we need to enable us to survive for one-hundred and twenty-six days?"

"Oxygen," said Charlie.

"The oxygen is mostly recycled, and so is the water, so we won't run out of oxygen and water."

"Good."

"What else do we need?"

"Food?"

"Yes, food."

"We've got enough, haven't we?" asked Charlie.

"To maintain life or to be comfortable?"

Charlie didn't respond. Then it dawned on him that he hadn't seen Steve eating anything other than the smallest of snacks. Steve said: "To be comfortable, we have enough food to last a month. If we ration it, to keep us at a point above starvation, we have enough to keep us going for about ninety days, depending on how strong we are."

"What about the pills?" asked Charlie.

"The calculations include the pills."

Charlie went very quiet. Steve continued: "We've got plenty of time to come up with a solution. Every problem has a solution. In fact, every problem has more than one solution."

"You must already have an idea then?" said Charlie.

"I do. In fact, I've got three ideas which might work, and which might get us home quicker, but I'm not going to share them with you until you've had enough time to think the problems through for yourself."

"Why not?"

"Because my ideas may be wrong, and you may come up with something I hadn't thought about. If I told you what I was thinking, you would naturally think along the same lines."

"If the worse came to the worse," said Charlie seriously, "and one of us had to be eaten, there's no point in eating me because I'm too skinny. I'm all skin and bone. See." He breathed in and showed his ribs.

"You're not skinny," said Steve. "You're perfectly fine for your age. I could cut two good steaks from your rump."

"Is that what it means *rump* steak?"

"Cow's bum."

Charlie grinned. "I'll never eat rump steak again."

"You will. And sooner than you think. I've got rump steak in the freezer. Anyway, in an attempt to take your mind off sinking your teeth into me, what other things in the cabin could provide the necessary carbohydrates, proteins and minerals?"

"Such as?"

"Think about it," said Steve.

Charlie looked around the cabin but his powers of observation and reason were numbed. He couldn't think of anything.

"Paper," said Steve.

"Paper?"

"Yes, where does it come from?"

"Trees."

"And trees are what?"

"Organic."

Steve opened a notebook and ran a finger along the flat of a page. "This wood pulp has been bled through with bleach but these notebooks could stave off hunger for a few days. Maybe a week. What else could we eat?"

Charlie looked around the cabin and again failed to come up with an answer. With some irritability he said: "I don't know. What's in the cupboards at the back?"

"You should know. You helped your Gran to pack them. But the thing I'm thinking of is in the cabin."

"Give me a clue."

"You're sitting on it."

"My rump?"

"The chair."

"The chairs?"

"They're leather. And leather comes from?"

"Cows bums."

"Hides, yes. But because of the tanning, I doubt these will be digestible."

Chapter 14

The eighth day inside the shuttle saw man and boy each with a note-pad on their lap. They had the same way of sitting, the same impressive air of concentration, and they held their pen in the same way. There were times when the pens moved left to right and up and down at the very same time, a remarkable feat even though they were doing very different calculations. A plan of action had been agreed upon and Charlie and Steve were doing the maths to see if the agreed plan was possible. Page after scribbled page flowed. And page after page proved that the plan was worth trying. They swapped notebooks and checked each other's calculations. After a meat and potatoes dinner late on the ninth day, Charlie was licking his plate clean when Steve asked what had he come up with?

"There is nothing on Earth, or in Earth's orbit, that can reach and rescue us," said Charlie.

"Correct."

"So, whatever we've got to do, we've got to do it ourselves."

"Correct. Good."

"The solar winds travel much faster than we are travelling at the moment."

"At nearly three million miles an hour, they do."

"But it would be difficult with this shuttle to find the right channel."

"Practically impossible," said Steve. "Worth a shot if it was our only chance, but if we did manage to hitch onto a solar wind, I doubt the shuttle would be sufficiently powerful to break free from it."

"We could harness the wind's power," said Charlie.

"How?"

"It's all just electrons whizzing about."

"Carry on," said Steve, curious.

"Harness the electricity in the atoms? They're already super-charged."

"They are, but we don't have the tools to do that here. What else have you come up with?"

"I know the ship generates power from solar cells in the covering."

"It does."

"I've noticed that the shuttle's wings are tucked away, unused at the moment. If the wings are also lined with solar cells they could be used to boost the shuttle's power and speed."

"They're not, so they can't, but well done. I hadn't thought of that. I'll certainly incorporate solar cells into the wings when we get back. You've earned a dessert. A chocolate bar?"

"No, thank you. It's best to save them until we don't need to."

"Good boy. Anything else?"

"The solar energy collected by the cells in the panelling is channelled into one main generator, and it is that generator which drives us forward."

"You're stating the obvious, but yes, go on. I'll give you a clue: Newton's Laws of Motion. You're on the right lines."

"We'll keep at the same speed until we get a push or a boost of additional power."

"In a vacuum, a body remains in a state of rest or uniform motion unless acted upon by an external force. Good."

"So we're going to keep moving at 5,800 miles an hour until something pushes us faster or slows us down."

"So, what can we do to the engine to make it produce more forward-thrusting power? It only needs a one-time surge," said Steve.

"Blow it up!" said Charlie. "We need to blow up the engine!"

"And what do we have on board that can cause an explosion?"

"Oxygen."

"And a limitless supply of hydrogen surrounding us. Now, what are the dangers we need to overcome?"

"We have to make sure we don't blow ourselves up. So the explosion has to take place outside the ship and it has to explode away from us.

Can you make the changes to the engine from inside the shuttle?"

"Not the physical changes."

"Which means a space walk."

"Which means we'll lose the oxygen already in circulation. So, if we are using our oxygen supplies to fuel the big bang, we have to make sure we have enough in reserve in case things go wrong."

"How much will we need?" asked Charlie.

"I don't know. We'll have to do the maths."

"Can we harness the hydrogen?"

"We'll have to. And we'll have to make sure that the explosion pushes away from the shuttle at a speed much greater than the one we're already travelling at. There's no point in having a five thousand mile-an-hour explosion if we're already travelling at five-thousand-eight-hundred." Steve paused before adding: "I don't suppose you know the speed at which oxygen explodes in a vacuum, do you? In combination with hydrogen?"

"No," said Charlie. "We didn't do that at school. Is hydrogen going to be the main component in the explosion?"

"A souped up hydrogen bomb. Yes."

"Then it's going to be big."

"A big, big, bang. I'll build a limiter and an appropriate compressor. That shouldn't be too difficult. But I'll have to dismantle the engine to get the parts. Now, what other safety concerns do we need to take care of?"

"Such as?"

"Stopping," said Steve.

"The solar cells in the front of the shuttle fire away from us to slow us down."

"They don't *fire*," said Steve, "but you're quite right. The only trouble is they've been built to stop a spaceship travelling at six thousand miles an hour, not one travelling at six hundred thousand, or whatever speed we're aiming for."

"Didn't you build any safety into them?"

"Yes, they're good for three or four times that, but that won't do for us. So we'll have to blow them up as well."

"Blow them up?"

"To stop us. We'll blow the engine at the back to send us forward. And blow the brakes in the front to slow us down. The ocean, of course, is our safety net, and not much of one, but with the wings out, acting as a sort of parachute, it's got a fair to middling chance of working. Are you ready to get to work?"

"Yes," said Charlie.

Much of the evening was spent making controlled explosions with oxygen. "Damn!" said Steve, blush-faced. "I've scorched the window. Look at that! I could have put the window through!"

Four days later, Charlie and Steve were still in very good spirits, but both reeked of a sweat built from anxiety, exhilaration and from simply not washing. The air recycling unit helped to ease the unpleasantness but the build up was more active than the clean up, so Charlie was secretly pleased when Steve spent most of the day outside the ship attached to an umbilical-like support cord. Outside, Steve dismantled and rebuilt the navigation unit, and he dismantled and rebuilt the engine. Charlie used the computer to monitor the re-installation processes. He was surprised by how simple it seemed. There was no drama and no dropped tools but it did take upwards of twelve hours. Then, after Steve had altered and shielded the breaks at the front of the ship, he returned to the spaceship exhausted. He detached himself from the support cord. It whipped itself back into its holding. He sealed the hatch and took off his helmet. "We've got one chance but two options."

"What?" said Charlie.

"Take off your helmet and you'll be able to hear me," said Steve, miming the actions. Charlie took off his helmet. "We've got one chance but two options. Option One, we light the fuse, the engine blows and gets us back to Earth in six weeks time, and we can eat and drink and be merry for some of that. We'll arrive thin and bearded but alive. Or, Option Two, we can crank it up and compress the explosion one notch further to provide more forward thrust, and we'll be home, or at least in the Atlantic Ocean, in less than an hour. Which do you want to do?"

"Is there any reason for not cranking it up?"

"The G-Force. The gravity-control unit inside the shuttle counteracts the G-Force, but if we crank it up we'll break the seal somewhat. It'll probably break in any case."

"How many Gs?" asked Charlie.

"Well, a good rollercoaster will put you under about 4Gs for about six seconds, and that is exhilarating. But our little booster back there, if switched from the nursery to the Big School setting, will give us nearly nine Gs at blast off, rising to nearly nineteen Gs for ninety seconds, at which point the wings will be released, and the brakes will start slowing us down."

"Will we black out?"

"I won't but you will."

"You mean *I* won't but *you* will."

Steve smiled. "So we go for the big one then?"

"Will the shuttle survive the impact?"

"It will, unless we're very unlucky and we hit a ship or a whale, or Ireland."

"What are the odds?"

"There's more sea than land."

"Let's give it a go," said Charlie. "Crank it up. Do you need to go back outside?"

"No, I've set it for the big one already."

Charlie grinned and picked up his helmet.

"It's actually safer without it on," said Steve. "There'll be less strain on your neck. Click it back on the rack and strap yourself in."

Charlie put the helmet back on the rack. They strapped themselves in. They closed the outside shutters. Charlie noticed a hesitation in Steve's actions, a barely perceptible slowness that Charlie had learned to mean that Steve was turning something over in his mind. Steve was thinking about the breaks. The breaks were shielded from the initial explosion, but he was worried that the force and the rattle may undo their effectiveness. Regardless of the setting, if the breaks failed, Steve knew that they would both be dead sixty seconds later.

"Steve? We'll be all right won't we?"

How does one mark the moment of one's death?

"Of course we will," said Steve, hoping to sound confident and reassuring. The chance of both of them surviving without having to blow up the engine to boost the speed was none at all. The chance of them surviving by blowing up the engine was less than two in ten thousand. And less than two in ten thousand beats zero in the game of life. The odds didn't shorten much if he switched the engine to the more gentle setting. Was that 'not much' worth it? It was. It wasn't. It was. It wasn't.

"Steve, what are you thinking about?"

Steve answered with: "Are you ready?"

Charlie nodded and said: "Yeah."

His own lack of confidence had undermined the boy's. The tone of Charlie's response made it clear to Steve that Charlie had seen through the delusive optimism. Something was needed to be done to lighten the mood. If they were going to die, and in all probability they were both going to die in the next couple of minutes, there was no point in doing it glumly. Steve undid his seatbelt, switched his seat to the toilet bowl setting, unloosened his trousers and sat back down. He said: "It's not that I'm afraid of crapping myself, Charlie, and in no way is this an attempt to disrespect The King, or to trivialise the circumstances of his death. You know how much he means to me. I love the guy. But if things go wrong, I don't think that, under the circumstances, it is too lacking in dignity for a man to die like Elvis Presley."

He pressed a button on the computer. The King of Rock and Roll starting singing *The American Trilogy*. "We started with The King. Let's end this royally."

Charlie screamed with laughter, undid his own seat belts and lowered his trousers. He altered his seat setting, and he used his hands to shape a quiff from his unwashed hair. "Do yours Steve! You've got to do your hair!"

Steve shaped his hair into a quiff. They looked at each other and laughed. With the King of Rock n' Roll now singing *Glory! Glory!*

Hallelujah!, Steve Atherton pressed the glory button, and the shuttle exploded forward at the very uncomfortable speed of twenty-one-million-miles-an-hour. Steve and Charlie were both laughing when the air was squeezed out of them.

Chapter 15

When Steve opened his eyes, he was in darkness broken only by pin lights on the control panel. He undid his seatbelt and pulled up his trousers. He pressed buttons on a panel above his head. The lights came on. Charlie, mouth agape, was unconscious but breathing soundly. With great carefulness, Steve checked Charlie's neck for injuries and, finding none, he undid the boy's seatbelts and pulled him up onto his shoulder. He pulled up the boy's trousers, returned the seat to the non-toilet setting, and sat him back down. He tried to open the outside shutters but they weren't working. He pulled wires from the wall and this woke the ship's computer. He opened the shutters and turned on the outside lights. He was surprised that some of them worked. The shuttle was on the silt-sand bottom of the Atlantic Ocean. More pulled wires, stripped and sparked, released and woke the ship's nautical engine. The shuttle rose from the bottom through a small whirl-cloud of colourless sand. Steve turned the craft, in accordance to settings now showing on the screen, and directed it upwards at a decompression angle so slight it would take them three hours before it surfaced.

With the craft now in motion, he checked Charlie's heartbeat and, finding it regular, he woke him gently. Charlie's nose started to bleed. "Pinch it on the bridge and stay calm. We're in the sea. We'll soon be home."

"Did I black out?"

"No, you were sleeping."

When the nose stopped bleeding, Steve used a tissue to clean Charlie's face. Charlie was silent for quite a while. He looked withdrawn. Damaged somehow. Or was that just Steve's imagination? Steve gave him a drink of water and told him to go to back to sleep. "I'll wake you when we surface. We'll be home soon. I'll wake you when it's time to wake up."

The shuttlecraft surfaced in daylight. Neither man nor boy had ever experienced anything as reviving as the iodine-rich sea air that flooded their lungs when they withdrew the hatch. With much ooing and ahhing they stood and stretched. "Each breath is a guinea in the bank of good health!" Both fell over comically when the low rolling sea made its first pass.

After a long and late afternoon at sea, they rounded the Irish coast two hours after sundown. They reached the Severn estuary eighty minutes after midnight. With the hatch now re-sealed, they re-submerged into the lifting tide to keep themselves safe from prying eyes as they travelled upstream. Tiredness was the main reason for their desire for anonymity. They hadn't the energy for the inevitable backpatting, praise, questions, concerns and greetings.

The shuttlecraft had lost a wing on re-entry and couldn't fly. Security would be breached if they were seen and followed. In the shallows where the river reached Gloucestershire, the roof of the shuttlecraft broke the surface and gleamed pearl-white in the night-black water, but the craft made it to the landing point without attracting attention. A night fisherman was the only one to see it, and then only briefly, his mind too occupied on domestic matters, and his impressive carp catch, to quite believe his eyes so he chose to ignore them. Untroubled he fished a full four hours more.

Steve and Charlie secured the shuttle at the top of a private landing ramp by a locked boat house owned by Charlie's grandfather. They would have put it inside the boat house but they couldn't find the key. They covered the shuttle with a tarpaulin sheet taken from another boat. They weighed the sheet down using river stones. When this task was complete, Charlie took his phone out of his backpack and started dialing numbers. Steve stopped him.

"I can get a signal here," said Charlie.

"Who are you calling?"

"Home."

'What time is it?"

Charlie looked at his phone and said, "4.13 am."

"What time do your grandparents go to bed?"

"Midnight."

"And if you Grandad misses his sleep what is he like in the morning?"

"In the morning? The whole week long, more like."

"And it is not just that, Charlie. It's wrong to inconvenience others unless it is an emergency. We're five miles from home. Six if you add in the hills, and it'll take us about two hours to walk it. If you are capable of walking for two hours we should walk it. You know we need the exercise. If you can't walk it, you can ring your grandparents."

Charlie turned off his phone.

"Is your leg okay? I've noticed you're limping a bit."

"It's okay," said Charlie, glumly.

With satchels on their backs containing their journals, the data discs, and everything else light enough and important enough to carry, Steve and Charlie began the night walk home. "We can take our time," said Steve. "If you start to struggle I'll carry you."

'There's no need of that."

At the end of the lane, they crossed a stile and took the long unlit pathway that began in the grassland of a limestone meadow and which rose, through covered lanes crowned with beech trees, to the remnants of a hill fort that overlooked the River Severn. They stopped for breath and drinks of water.

"Stop sulking, Charlie."

"I'm not sulking."

They re-shouldered their packs and continued on in silence. To Charlie, the sound of everything was heightened. He hadn't realised before how noisy silence was. Perhaps it was a sign that he was ill?

His legs felt weak. His body hurt. He hoped he was ill. That would teach Steve a lesson.

Ten minutes short of two hours later, they arrived at Steve Atherton's house on the green across from the house where Charlie lived. There was more than an hour before Grandad's waking time, and Charlie was almost out on his feet, so he was granted the rare treat of staying at Steve's house. The boy now eased to bed after a quick hot dish of defrosted beef casserole and three glasses of cold tap water. Though inwardly as excited about the new surroundings as he had been about almost anything he had seen and done on the journey to Mars, Charlie slept quickly and soundly, unaware that Steve spent the remaining night hours clearing up the mess caused by the government break-ins.

On entering the house, Charlie had glimpsed the sitting room scattered with papers and this had surprised him because he had known Steve only to be fastidious. "Oh, it's been blown about by the open window. Silly me," said Steve, ushering Charlie out of the room and guiding him away from the back room in anticipation of an equally upsetting sight there. The kitchen and the second bedroom were as neat as Steve had left them. With Charlie exhausted and relaxing into sleep almost as soon as he stepped across the threshold, it was easy to keep him away from the room with the open window. Except that the window wasn't open it was smashed, as was the crystal trophy Steve had won as a young scientist at Cambridge, and two picture frames that once held treasured images of his own childhood. There was a boot crease across the photograph of his mother face.

Chapter 16

The return from Mars was not announced to the world until Steve and Charlie both felt strong enough to face it. On the third day back, Charlie fainted from a build-up of stress and fatigue, and was prescribed a prolonged bed rest by Grandma. This prompted Charlie's grandfather to take ill to his bed out of sympathy. Grandma wasn't pleased. In the comforting knowledge that both of them could hear her, she repeatedly complained loudly that this was "the last time" she would "allow herself to be taken advantage of" (meaning nurse them), whilst knowing wholeheartedly that it wouldn't be. Hers had been a lifetime of caring for the weaker sex. "I'm not selfish enough to get ill," was one of her sayings. Husband and grandson she nursed with equal severity and effectiveness and love.

Eight days after returning home, Steve and Charlie faced the world's media at a press conference in the ballroom of a Cheltenham hotel. The management were practiced in the art of getting people in and out undetected. Charlie gave Steve a gift of a pair of dark glasses. "I bought these for you."

"What's this?"

"I bought them when I was Grandma," said Charlie, putting on an identical pair. "Do I look good?"

"Yes. They fit you this time."

"So, what you're saying is, I looked ridiculous last time?"

"You did," said Steve. "But what could I do? We were pushed for time."

Charlie laughed and, with both hands, gave Steve a playful push in the back, moving him towards the guarded door. The guard opened the door. There were cheers and applause and a lot of people pushing. There was a lot of noise. Steve put on the glasses and said: "Let's go and get our eyeballs flashed out."

PART TWO
THE PHILOSOPHERS

The theme of Grandad's latest public lecture was Happiness. It drew an audience so large that it had to be moved from the village hall to the village green, with Grandad's words amplified by a microphone and speakers, and his person made easier to see by an improvised stage consisting of a table collected from his garden shed. He was in a bad mood afterwards. His grumpy bad temper reared itself with the sound of applause still ringing in everyone's ears and it continued all the way through supper. The temper surprised those closest to him, and their surprise disappointed him because it meant that they had not listened properly to the lecture. On that stage, on that green, he told in words most carefully chosen that *constructed stability* was the only route to happiness. How could he be happy when his constructed plans had been torn apart by the change of venue brought about by an unexpected crowd who had gathered mostly to catch a glimpse of Charlie? He knew they were there to look at the boy and not at him and, in truth, that didn't bother him. But it bothered him that they didn't seem to listen. It bothered him that his family hadn't listened. And it bothered him that the crowd didn't seem to go away. They stayed for days.

"Why are they here, Grandad?"

"Some-are-born-to-endless-night," said Grandad wistfully. "What boring lives they must lead. Some of them haven't moved from the garden gate for three days now. Do they not have friends or families?"

"What is Grandma saying to them?"

"We can switch on the TV to find out, but it's rude to pry. She'll tell us later if she wants us to know." He looked closely at his grandson. "Would you feel up to it if she asked you to go out there and speak to them? It could help to move things along?"

"No," said Charlie skulking away from the window. He sat down on the floor with his back to the wall. "I'm completely worn out."

"The police patrol will be up and running before seven, so we'll be able to sleep tonight."

At seven o'clock, Officers Alva and Adams arrived in a marked car spinning its siren lights and broadcasting their arrival. Their forceful but courteous manner, which included much repetition of the phrases *Public Nuisance Order, Nothing to See* and *Time to Go Home*, cleared most of the crowd from the front of the house; a fixed penalty notice served to a London reporter, followed by a lick of the pen and the announcement, '*Who's Next? Form an Orderly Queue*", cleared the rest.

After tipping their caps in Grandad's direction, they stationed their car on the village green in sight of both Charlie's house and the house where Steve Atherton lived. Their no loitering policy worked well. "An arrest a day keeps trouble at bay," said Alva, as the doors closed on a back-up van called in to carry away a photographer they found hiding in a tree. Day by day, the efficiency of Alva and Adams helped them to become less busy, with the result that the night shift became a time for quiet contemplation, stolen naps, and philosophical discussion: "No, no, no. No, no, no, no, no," said officer Adams. "Elton John did a good job at Diana's funeral so I'll never hear a bad word said against him. He can certainly put on a show but he's not Elvis Presley. He's not Tom Jones or Mick Jagger. He can't ever achieve their levels of perfection in performance because he is missing the essential ingredient."

"The black gene?"

"That's right. It's the Yin and the Yang. The black seed in the white egg. The white seed in the black egg. It's Muhammed Ali, Cassius Clay. Do you understand what I'm saying?"

"No."

"Where does mankind come from?"

"What?"

"You know, in the beginning. Where do we come from?"

"Aliens."

Adams expressed his displeasure. "We're not from aliens."

"Aliens mated with apes and taught us how to use a wheelbarrow."

"A wheelbarrow?"

"And ride horses. Then we built the pyramids."

After gasps of exasperation, Adams said: "*Africa.* The first man was *African.* Some people say it was the Middle East, but God gave up on the Middle East. He drowned everyone except the Noahs and started again in Turkey. Sometime after that, Christ was born in Bethlehem."

"Is that why we have turkey at Christmas?"

"I'm trying to have a serious discussion here."

"Sorry."

"Christ was born in Bethlehem in the Middle East but the human race started in Africa. Thousands of years before that."

"You know that for a fact?"

"I do, yes. We started in Africa, or it might have been Portugal. In any case, we were in Africa before there was water in the Red Sea. And we were black. The first man was black. The man that God made was black. Therefore the one perfect man, made from the clay of God by God was black. So you can't have perfection in man without the black gene. That's why Elvis was King. He was born in the Mississippi swamplands of a Black America transported there in chains from Africa, and he was imbued with the rhythms and the voices of a black line that went right back to Genesis. When Elvis sang, his singing reached back to that first and true perfection, the clay of God, and every woman in the room wanted to mate with him. That's not an intellectual decision on their part it's something in the ether, something to do with The Spirit of the Clay. Do you see what I'm getting at? It's the Yin and the Yang. Tom Jones had it. Tom Jones is a black man who happens to have white skin. The Yin and the Yang. Put a thousand women in a room with Tom Jones and the essence of the genesis of man happens all over again. A thousand women go berserk and take off their knickers. You have to be black-white or white-black to have that shot of perfection."

"Don't you mean black-black. If the first and only perfect man, the one from God's clay, was black. Then the perfect man is black."

Adams frowned. "You've got a point. I need to think this through again."

There was a knock on the car window. Both men jumped and put a hand to their heart. It was Steve Atherton holding a tray of tea and bacon sandwiches. He sometimes started his long days of work at the Bat Cave by delivering small thank you gifts to the police officers. He was grateful for their presence and protection. He was grateful too for the continuing patronage of Charlie's grandfather to whom he had assigned the rights of the Martian film footage. It meant he was able to reject all governmental and all public and private offers of support for his continuing projects, together with the unworkable compromises that the involvement of others would bring. The money poured in and poured out. More titanium, more components, more hardware, more leather. A new spacecraft was being designed and built. "Is the leather edible?" asked Steve. The saleswoman looked aghast. "Not that I'm going to eat it. I was just wondering if it was organic? I mean, I want leather chairs that are as natural as can be."

Chapter 18

Five weeks after the press conference, Charlie slid down the Bat Pole, entered the cave and found Steve at work in the laboratory. An electric hum; a loud snapping noise; a streak of bouncing purple light and a shower of sparks. When Steve saw Charlie, he turned off the machine. "Charlie, good to see you. You've arrived at a good time."

"Why? Have you built the forcefield?"

"No, because it's time for a break. Let's go to the kitchen and make a pot of tea. I've got some of those caramel slices we both like. And you can tell me all about the troubles you're having at school."

This surprised Charlie. He said: "How do you know I'm having trouble at school?"

"Because the school day ended ten minutes ago, and you could not have got from school to here in ten minutes."

A rush of pink coloured Charlie's cheeks.

"There's no need to be embarrassed, Charlie. I'm not telling you off. I think you've done well to stick it out this far, presuming this is your first day off?"

The boy lowered his eyes.

"Well, don't worry about that," said Steve.

"She'll call me *n.b.*"

She was Charlie's grandmother. *n.b.* was short for naughty boy, because 'naughty boys never make anything of themselves. They're footnotes to the narrative of life.'

Steve gave Charlie's head a gentle rub. "I was against you going back at all, Charlie. And there's no need to look guilty, and there's no need to sulk. And I don't want you throwing a tantrum when I say this, but I think your school days are over. Yes. Over. Now, stop smiling and put your grumpy face back on until we've worked out what we need to say to your Grandmother. Oh, before we do, were you followed coming here?"

"Of course," said Charlie.

"The American?"

"Yes."

"Where did you lose him?"

"The woods."

"The entrance?"

"Yes, before the first oak."

"Good boy. Let me show you my new toy."

He took Charlie to a side room.

"Screen on," said Steve.

The wall-screen came on and showed the upper outside entrance to the cave. "Human life," said Steve. The screen split into three equal sections. There were human beings in the three sections. "If there were twenty groups of people in the woods, the screen would split into twenty."

"How many cameras are there?"

"Twenty," said Steve. "There's your man." The man on the screen was wearing a panama hat, a tailored suit and a fistful of rings.

"Never trust a man who wears more than one ring," said Steve.

"Unless he's an artist. The rules are different for artists."

"He's not an artist," said Charlie. "Who are the other people?"

"That's Cedric. He finished installing the cameras yesterday. He works for your Grandad. I'm surprised you don't know him?"

"I do know Cedric. I just didn't recognise him on the screen."

"Who are they?" asked Steve, pointing to two boys engaged in an act of minor vandalism, probably in preparation for building a den or a treehouse.

"Russell and Paul. They're from my school," said Charlie.

"Friends?"

"No."

"Let's see if we can get a closer look at your American friend. This is the first time I've tried this. I hope it works. Take a head map of Sector One." The screen image of the American turned into a three-dimensional line-drawing. The drawing rotated on the screen and zoomed in until the front outline of the head filled the screen.

"That's good," said Charlie.

Concentrating on the screen, Steve said. "I.D. match." The three-dimensional drawing moved to the upper left corner of the screen where it weaved out photographs of twenty-two people. The twenty-two photographs now filled the screen in straight rows.

"Where did you get the images from?" asked Charlie.

"The internet," said Steve, still looking at the screen. "Identical matches." The photographs disappeared. "That means that's not his real face."

"Or he's not on the internet," said Charlie.

"Probable matches," said Steve to the screen. Nine images returned to the screen. "Identifications." Beneath each photograph came dates, names, occupations, identification marks, addresses. Steve scanned through the information, increasing and reducing the size of the text as he read.

"He can't be that one," said Charlie. "That's a woman."

"I'm not satisfied he's any of them," said Steve. "Which makes him more dangerous than I thought."

"Why?"

"Because he or his employers must have similar software to this and they've erased him from cyberspace."

Charlie asked: "Where did you get the software?"

"It's tweaked from a fairly standard Anglo-American defence project. Which means he probably works for the Anglo-American defence."

"You don't work for the Anglo-American defence."

"And I didn't pay for it *quid pro quo* like they wanted me to. I paid hard cash."

"Why don't you just have him arrested?"

"Because he hasn't broken the law," said Steve.

"He grabbed me."

"He didn't *grab* you. He put a hand on your shoulder and said, 'Hello'. That's not breaking the law. He could perfectly reasonably argue that he was being sociably human. There was a time when being Sociably Human was a good thing."

"But there's something about him that's wrong."

"Apart from the hat? He's dressed so loudly as to qualify for Hide in Plain Sight."

"There was no emotion in his eyes," said Charlie.

"PC Adams and Alva have had a talk with him, Charlie. We've got our eye on him."

"Isn't he trespassing?"

"Not really. Your Grandad owns the land but it's registered as public ground."

"Why?"

"To keep us hidden."

"Are you going to zap him?"

"If he takes the wrong turn at that fork I'm going to have to press a few buttons." The American took the wrong turn. Charlie grinned. Steve pressed buttons. The area of forest into which the American had wandered was known locally as the Dark Acres and consisted mostly of an unnaturally dense belt of black alder, hazel and hawthorn. The trees overhead hid the tricks below that shaped and re-shaped the forest paths. Buttons pressed in the control room of the Bat Cave altered the pathways with new interweavings of

spiked fauna and risings of bog water and mud. The only way out
was to go back the way you came in. All attempts to enter the Dark
Acres from another position were met with subtly changing barriers.
With the hydraulic and hydrating changes now taking place,
Steve turned off the screens, for he took no pleasure in inflicting
frustration and pain, or in watching the results. He said: "Now, let's
go and have that pot of tea, and sort out that problem of yours."

"Oh, that," said Charlie.

"Yes, that," said Steve.

The problem was that nobody at school could quite believe that
Charlie Ellis was the same boy they'd known for years. Everyone now
treated him differently. The once popular boy was now regarded as
a freak. Teachers made cutting remarks about his achievements
and fame, others condescended him with overdone smiles.

"All of them?"

"No, Mr. Keane, the History teacher is alright. The rest are barely
human."

"Teachers are trained to be sub-human, Charlie, so I know your
problem isn't with the teachers." The problem was with Charlie's
fellow pupils. They fell into two groups. Those who were starstruck
into stupidity: "You know, giggling and pointing and whispering."

The other group thought it was cool to ignore him.

"Ignore you?"

"Turn their back on me, literally. In science, for example, if anyone
sits next to me, the rest of the class think they're sucking up and
so won't speak to that person except to make threatening remarks.
Then, of course, at breaktime, that person ignores me too to prove
to the class that they're not sucking up."

"How dreadfully childish. These people were your friends?"

"I thought so. And they deliberately walk into me in the corridor
and things."

"How long has this been going on?"

"Since Day One."

"Why didn't you tell me before?"

"I didn't think it was important. It was not as if I was being beaten up or anything. I thought it would sort itself out."

"Have you talked to your teachers about it?"

"Not really."

"Do you still cycle to school?"

"Yes. But there's the police car outside the school and another at the top of the hill."

"The police are there for you, Charlie."

"I know. Perhaps that's part of the problem?"

"I knew you'd be bullied. There is something in the British character that hates success. And I know there's nothing I can do to stop it," said Steve. "Which is why you can never go back."

"Why can't you stop it?"

"Because it's the natural behaviour of low people retarded by a system that exists to keep them retarded. We can only beat the bullies by changing the system. And I'm too selfishly busy to do that."

"Is it because they're jealous of me?"

"Not really," said Steve, making the tea. "Jealousy plays a part, but the social and emotional skills of your fellow pupils are so retarded that they don't really know what they think about you, because they don't really think at all. They've been stunted by an enforced lack of self-discipline and by an almost complete and total absence of a sense of self-responsibility. Intentionally, or otherwise, bad schools, such as yours, suppress the growth of responsibility because they were set up to produce an obedient workforce drilled into accepting a life of monotony. To that end, everything is dictated down from the top, from the government to the headmaster, to the management, to the teachers, with the result that no one in the system, teachers as well as pupils, develops a proper sense of responsibility. How can they take full responsibility for their actions when their actions are dictated to them by others?"

Charlie bit into a caramel slice. Steve poured the tea.

"But there are good schools aren't there?"

"I hope so, but even the good ones are being rotted from the inside by the culture of conformism. For example, ten years ago, at your Grandad's request, I went to visit his old school to see about the possibility of him and your parents sending you there when you were old enough. Because it took almost a full day to get there, I'd been invited to stay the night. My contact was a housemaster called Jennings, a man I'd never met. I arrived at the school at about 9pm and found a notice pinned on Jennings' door which said: 'Dear Mr. Atherton, sorry not to be here when you arrived, but I was offered Covent Garden tickets too good to miss. I'll be back after midnight. The boys will look after you.' Two Sixth Form boys, about eighteen years old, asked who I was, and invited me to join them in the common room where they made me a pot of tea and gave me supper, cooking it on a full stove in the corner."

"What did you have?"

"That's not important. Over the next hour or so, the common room filled with other boys, all of them polite and industrious, talking intelligently among themselves or with me, or busying themselves with a book or their studies. Or making something to eat. Relaxing and laughing. At about ten o'clock, a younger-looking boy arrived and announced that the third and fourth formers were all in bed and were quiet and the lights had been turned out. Some time after midnight, Mr. Jennings arrived back and invited me and the two boys he'd left in charge to have a whiskey with him in his study. That was the system that had thrived for hundreds of years, turning out generations of industrious responsible men like your Grandad."

"That's not what it's like at my school," said Charlie.

"Your mother didn't want you to go to boarding school. A couple of years ago, I was invited back to your Grandad's old school to give a lecture. I was shocked by the changes brought in by a weak headmaster schooled only in the latest educational fads, and who had allowed himself to be bullied by the media into accepting a string of imbecilic government-ordered reforms. A case of bullying all the teachers because one or two of them had misbehaved. Again I stayed in Jenning's house. He told me he had applied for early retirement because the school was no longer in the business of making responsible men. In the interest of safety, and the perverse goal to eliminate risk, the headmaster had decided that anything and everything that carried the now dirty tags of risk and responsibility had to be done by staff members and not by the boys. The staff, now burdened with a whole host of additional duties, were overworked to the point where they became second-rate masters and mentors. The Upper Sixth, stripped of the serious privilige of responsibility, now spent their evenings not in the common room, or in the tutoring and supervision of the younger boys, but in the pubs in town. The only ways left for them to show that they were becoming men was to show off how much they could drink, and how many girls they could chase."

The difficulties Charlie was having at school were not replicated at the scout meetings he attended, and which took on a new importance when Grandma gave him permission to withdraw from school, because they were now the only time he spent in the company of boys. The success of Charlie's continuing involvement in scouting was due to the skill and foresight of the scout leader improbably called Slim (for he was a large man). When Charlie arrived at the Scout Hut on the Wednesday after the Cheltenham press conference, the other boys crowded him excitedly and questioned him about the Martian adventure. Charlie answered their questions. They asked more questions. He answered them too. The scout leader let this continue for as long as it took the boys to have their fill. But, of course, boys do not all reach their fill at the same time, so Slim kept a close eye on the proceedings. When the introductory welcome became a twenty-minute crowd-and-talk, Slim asked the two assistants to go to the kitchen and make the troop some cocoa. He eased the group into the hall where, talking, listening, laughing, they sat on the floor in a horseshoe formation around Charlie. Slim noticed that Simon, the brightest and second eldest patrol leader, was becoming restless. Simon was at the stage of his development where he needed to be the centre of attention. This was to cover for a lack of self-confidence at the root of which was the belief that his penis was too small.

After forty minutes, with the distraction of the distribution of the cocoa - "Biscuits too, Bryan. There are a couple of tins in the end cupboard to the left of the sink" - Slim eased his way into the conversation and, with an invisible skilfulness acquired from nearly thirty years of working with boys, he brought it, on the hour, to a satisfactory close. He then asked Simon to lead the troop in a competitive team game he knew all the boys enjoyed, and which would therefore take their thoughts and pressures away from Charlie.

After the game, and with the meeting still with a full twenty-minutes to run, Slim gathered the troop together for the closed-eye silence of prayers. The troop always responded well to Slim's prayers because they respected him. Lacking a preacher's pomposity, Slim's prayers took the boys upwards to where their spirits dwelt. His prayers made the boys feel good about themselves, and about the community in which they lived, and the world and the God that they served. Amen. And Slim knew it would undo all his good work, and embarrass Charlie, if he mentioned Charlie in his prayers, so he didn't mention him. He knew never to spotlight individuals because he knew that everyone was equal. No one was more deserving or less deserving of God's attention. He knew that Charlie was as important as Simon, and that Simon was as important as the two new boys he would invite to join the troop next week. He would visit the new boys' parents tomorrow and bring forward their introduction and investiture by six weeks. This would help to keep the troop focused on scouting matters, and it would take the pressure away from Charlie.

Slim's scout programmes were always good, an interlacing mix of the physical, the social, the intellectual and the spiritual, but he would keep his assistants behind after tonight's meeting so they could look again at the programme they had planned for the coming weeks. With them, he would see what could be done to improve it, and what could be done to accommodate Charlie's special needs. He knew that Charlie was in danger of losing his childhood. Slim would do everything in his power to alleviate that danger.

Chapter 19

Grandad was lying on his bed indulging his morbid passion for the void and thinking of the day twenty or more years ago when Steve Atherton came into his life, knocking on his door, after all that excitement at the lake. He was hating himself for trying to find fault with Steve, and he was hating himself for failing to find fault. Feeling not unlike King Henry, who had cried of Becket, "Who will rid me of this troublesome priest?", he was weighing up the whys and wonts and feeling very sorry for himself. 'He's a good man through and through and I wish he'd left me alone. I wish he had never been and never was. I wish he'd go away'.

This surly almost private condemnation, for nothing under Grandma's roof could ever truly be called private, was the result of an ill-temper caused by the change in the routine brought about by Charlie's withdrawal from school.

At first, Grandad tired himself out by busying around to make himself useful to Charlie. At the kitchen table he'd give history *talks*, for he didn't know how to *teach*, on topics close to his heart. From the attic, he pulled out old schoolbooks, mostly mathematics, from the first post-war curriculum, and geography books in which most of the world was coloured pink. After two weeks, he started taking longer to get up in the morning. His mood darkened and he started to kick the furniture and complain about a pain in his chest. Now he was privately grumbling about a man he'd raised almost since boyhood and whom, in times of better moods, had been his pride and joy. Then the tutors came, or *Those Dreadful People* as Grandad called them. He couldn't stand the sight of them. He hated to see and hear strangers in his house. He loathed the way they stared at the famous boy. Some had high hopes and impressive recommendations but none of them seemed right. The worst talked an ugly academic jargon of key skills and attainment levels and assessment points.

"Poor thing," said Grandma, "doesn't she know she sounds like a machine?"

Barely more impressive were the foreign students looking for a way to subsidize their own studies. A Polish girl called Eva caught Grandma's eye, but more on account of her nationality than her abilities. Grandma herself was proudly Polish. "We'll give her another chance, Charlie. See if she spends the week planning lessons. She's a nice girl. Don't you think?"

"She was okay," he said with a frown.

But Eva didn't spend the week planning lessons.

"Well, at least there's Steve."

On Friday afternoons, Steve came round to teach science and to report on his week's work. He often brought what Grandma called his bag of tricks. His science lessons, attended by all three members of the household, sometimes took the form of Steve demonstrating innovations he was planning for the new spaceship. A few minor disasters left him blush-faced and apologetic. "Oh, don't worry about that," said Grandma. "The sparks were as pretty as a firework, and the wall, I'm sure, can be fixed."

Most afternoons, Charlie could be found at the Bat Cave, working away with dignity and a good deal of noise. Everywhere around him were tools, sheets of titanium and copper, half-finished jobs. Most evenings, he studied the Seven Unconquered Planets, or SUPS as he and Steve had started calling them. "Have you Supped?" and "I've been Supping" became stock phrases in their private jargon. Charlie studied weather systems, chemistry, geology and star charts. He made and approved designs and he checked calculations.

In the autumn, Steve made a rare visit to Russia to meet a research team who claimed to have engineered a new type of telescope, but the subtext of the visit was to protest about the fines and harrassments he was getting at home from the central government. The harrassment which started with the break-in was swiftly followed by a trumped up fine and the threat of a prison sentence for threatening national security for flying round Big Ben.

Steve's refusal to share his secrets with the military brought in an almost weekly post-drop of regulatory complaints and fines. He let it be known that if the government didn't back down he would start sharing his secrets with Russia. This approach rattled proud doors in Westminster and so bruised the egos of politicians and their corporate paymasters that they backed a public hate campaign through the press. The press were keen to turn on Steve Atherton, because he wouldn't play their game of celebrity, but they had held back their venom because the public barometer held strongly in Steve's favour.

"We're not asking you to do your worst, exactly," said the Minister's under-secretary, at a meeting of men and women whose morals were so low they would probably sell their own colleagues for the price of a cup of tea, "but just enough to let him know how you feel. It's time for a change in the wind."

So when the press wind started to blow, Steve Atherton stepped off the plane in Moscow, to sunshine skies and to crowds that would have stunned The Beatles. In the three weeks he spent with the Russian scientists, he improved their telescope beyond the point of impossibility, for he knew that when it came to power, big meant small. "Have you not tried making it smaller?" asked Steve, a careful hand on the silver casing.

"This is the optimum size," said the second-in-command. "It is impossible to shave off even a fraction of an inch."

"So, I take it you haven't tried atomic compression?" The group looked at him blankly. "Show me your workroom. I'll show you what I mean."

In Steve's absence, Grandad rose from his bed to take full control of Charlie's education. He prepared what he called a Father and Son talk, a birds and the bees thing, after noticing that Charlie had reached an age when it would be sensible to know such things. But after arranging for Grandma to be out of the house, and after doing a lot of coughing and throat-clearing and arm-swinging, he decided instead that what the boy really needed was a lesson on Ethics and Power. He considered himself an authority on these subjects because he believed that he always did the right thing, and because he had a benign but almost total control over the local government. This unsought power had formed naturally because the local councillors knew they could not function as effectively without his patronage, and were wise enough and humble enough to recognise that fact. For decades, Grandad's wealth and good sense had been a quiet fixer behind the scenes. There wasn't an aspect of local public life, from road building to farming, medicine, schools, the arts and the police, that did not benefit from Grandad's gentle generosity. When local budgets had been spent, there was always Grandad and his loyal workforce ever ready to fix a roof, back a show and clean up after a flood.

"Do for the doing, not for the praise, and spend your money wisely. That means don't give it to someone else to spend for you. If, for example, a headmaster contacts the office and asks for £20,000 to fix the teachers' carpark, then I pay my own workmen to fix the teacher's carpark. If I gave the headmaster the £20,000, and he's one of the most trustworthy men in public office, then he'll spend a quarter of it on *administration costs*, whatever that means, and another quarter on this and that, and the carpark will be fixed on the cheap by a cheap contractor and will need re-doing in a year or two. A pound spent wisely is a pound spent by yourself on others. Remember, there are no rich men in Heaven, and no poor ones too if you catch your Grandmother on one of her bad days. How long have I been talking?"

Charlie looked at the clock to the left of the kitchen table. "Twelve minutes."

"Twelve? And your lesson is how long? Twenty?"

"An hour, you said. But twenty's plenty."

"Twenty it is then, but we'll mark it down for an hour. Where was I up to?"

"You started off by talking about Ethics, which means 'doing the right thing', and you got up to the bit about there being no rich men in Heaven, and no poor ones."

"Right. Erm...", Grandad took a deep breath and straightened his back, having become conscious of the fact that he had stooped to hear what Charlie was saying. Then he said: "A good deed is only good if it is done properly. The workers and the materials have to be top drawer. People come to me because they know I do things properly. Part of the doing-things-properly is the part that says 'Don't pat your own back and don't bang your own drum'. Drum-banging reduces your effectiveness as a good man because it frightens the more sensitive people away. It's unethical to boast. Are you writing this down?"

"Yes, Grandad."

Chapter 20

The press attacks on Steve Atherton were not particularly successful. The majority of the public were unswayed. They knew the difference between a man of real achievement and a rude lot of hot air. And the newspaper editors were reluctant to press their nails into the boy. Sales fell a bit. Advertisers withdrew partially, so it was a relief to the editors when the Nobel Prize committee rang a big Norwegian bell for Steve Atherton, by awarding him a share of a Prize for his work on what became known as the Atherton telescope. When, later, Steve took delivery of the body of the new spaceship, he fitted it with two Atherton telescopes, one of which was later tweaked to see into the heart of Creation itself.

The American press started singing Steve Atherton's praises because the American science community got their hands on their own Atherton telescope. Steve was relaxing in his office in the Bat Cave, reading the newspapers and journals, and feeling a little giddily proud of such public approval, page after page of praise for the dawning of The Age of The New Miracles of Science and All Hail to The Great Man of the Moment - Steve Atherton. The ring-fingered American in Roeminster even stopped scowling at the old ladies who seemed to follow him everywhere and whom he knew had been sent to spy on him by Charlie's Grandmother.

But not everyone was impressed. The least impressed of all was a thirteen-year-old boy called Charlie Ellis: "Did you really give away the secret of atomic compression?" said Charlie dumbfounded and edging towards a tantrum. "How *could* you be so *stupid*?"

"Stupid? I was being clever," said Steve. "By giving them a leg up into the next level of science, I was tying up scientific research there and in America for the next twenty or thirty years. I knew the Russians would leak and sell everything to the States. And they did. Look!" He held up a newspaper. "Though I didn't expect it to be so quick and so complete. I couldn't have done it the other way round because the Americans would not have sold out to the Russians. As it is, the Russians are happy. The Americans are happy. The papers are happy."

"And I'm not happy at all!"

"Charlie, that little bit of new knowledge will give them so much work to do they won't be bothered in bothering us. The governments will pour money into science. Men and women will bring home the bacon and lots of clever kids will be put through school. I've sprinkled a bit of gold dust. Given them a stepping stone. I doubt they can take the next step. Stop scowling at me."

"*If* they have the secret to atomic compression, *which-they-have!* they have the means to break the fabric of the universe. You've said so yourself."

"I know I have. But they won't get that far. I know them. They'll need to keep producing results, so they'll be so sidetracked by the new bells and whistles that they'll miss the bigger picture."

"They'll be furious when they find out that atomic compression isn't particularly linked to space travel. That's what they are after."

"I know it is. We'll come to that hurdle when it happens, oh, in probably ten or twenty years time. They'll never crack the secret. Charlie. I've bought us some breathing space. A lot of breathing space. Don't you see that? Did you not sense that the noose was closing in? It was. Trust me. It was. And I've cut the rope. Won back our freedom. You can pat me on the back if you want to?" He turned his right shoulder and showed his back to Charlie.

"You've opened a playground for psychopaths."

"It was a moral decision," Charlie. "I did it to protect us. Man's a moral animal. We live and die by the decisions we make."

Charlie's eyes flashed with a rare anger. He knew his safety had been compromised on the Martian adventure. A bad command to a poorly programmed computer had come close to killing him. Rare was the night when he didn't dream about meteorites and wet his sheets with his sweat. He was tempted to blurt out and cause an even bigger scene. Instead he lowered his eyes and said: "Sorry."

But something inside him had changed. It would take him a while to recover his full admiration and trust for Steve Atherton. He knew that Steve was the most brilliant of all men, and a good man through and through, but he'd been thinking about it recently, and was surprised and disappointed to have to conclude that Steve was proving to be a weaker man than he should be. Charlie knew that he could have survived a hundred days and more inside the shuttlecraft. The mathematics didn't add up to survival but he knew that mathematics didn't always equate with real life. He knew in his bones that he would have lived in that closed capsule for three hundred days if he had to, and he had sensed that Steve was not as full of the fight of life as he was. And that disappointed him. He was disappointed too that Steve had given in to government pressures so quickly and so completely. Grandad could have took them on and Grandma could have shouted them down. Charlie Ellis had been brought up to know the difference between actions and words. Steve had spent years saying one thing, and now he had done the opposite of what he'd been saying all along. So went the strands of Charlie's thoughts.

Steve Atherton was sufficiently aware of his own failings to refuse to green light the SUP project, or to sign off Charlie's final designs for Spaceship 2, until he'd made a forcefield, or deflector shield, that could keep them safe from everything the universe could throw at them. "That was rubbish. We were closer than that two months ago," said Charlie, of the latest failed experiment. "What's the thinking behind the thing?"

"Good to see you've cheered up," said Steve. "As you know, a force-field is a barrier that is impossible to penetrate. To make a barrier that cannot be penetrated by anything we must build one that prevents even atomic transfer. I've given up on the idea of a Faraday Cage. The only way I can think of to stop the inter-reaction of atoms is to bind them together in a way that doesn't alter their structure."

"So?"

"Well, I know that doesn't sound difficult, and I've found more than one way of doing it, but the difficulty is having sufficient control over it so it can be turned on and turned off."

"So? The answer is in the power source."

"I'm sure it is, but I'm learning that it isn't."

Chapter 21

In the police car on the green, two men were deep in conversation: "It's why the S.S. wore black uniforms. Do you see? It was a corrupted black skin that imbued them with some kind of corrupted black power. The Yin in a Yang's cloak. You know? Like when you pull on a red Liverpool shirt when you go for a game of football, even just a kick about on the park. There is a power in the colour of the cloth. It makes you a better footballer. It links you to a different energy. When you put on a red shirt you become Kenny Dalglish. Do you see what I'm getting at?"

"I think so. It's true there's some kind of transformation."

"It's why we wear uniforms. Well, one of the reasons. I'm not making value judgements about white men being this and black people being that. I've done some reading since our last conversation, and the colour of our skin is determined solely by the birthplace of our genes *geo-graphi-cally*. If they are born on the sunny Equator your skin will be deep black. If they are born in the lands without sun, or with very little sun, then you will be Scot-ginger, but I think the colours must have different energies, different properties, and that to achieve perfection you have to have the energies from more than one colour, or actually, from all of the colours. That's it! My God, I've cracked it. Perfection is a rainbow!"

"You're losing me."

"The secret to life has something to do with colour. Coloured light. No. That's not it. A rainbow is all the visible colours of light. In reality they're seperate. You have to combine them to make perfect light."

"How do you know all this stuff?"

"It must be something in the water. These thoughts come to me at night."

"The first thing that God created was light," said Charlie.

"It was," said Steve. "If you are talking about the story of the creation of Man."

Steve Atherton had been experimenting with coloured light in an attempt to break open the secrets to light speed. In his teens, in a brand new work room given to him by Grandad, he had written in chalk on a blackboard: 'Everything can go faster than the speed of light except light itself'. Then he set about proving that theory. With a few tweaks of quite ordinary mathematics, he found that this anti-Einsteinian hope could be made to work on paper. But how to make it work in practise? He knew that the easiest way to travel at light speed was to travel within the light itself, but hooking oneself onto light beams was easier said than done. He was lucky in that he instinctively made the right decision to use only natural light in his experiments. That meant harnessing the sun. "The answer to all our questions lies within it or comes from it because it is the tool of our Creation. It was the light of our beginning. It's no wonder that even Heraclitius looked upon it as a god. But then he did have the advantage of being closer to the time of Creation, fifteen hundred years unclouded by man-made obfuscation. And the sun solves the mystery of which came first, the chicken or the egg."

"What are you talking about?" said Charlie Ellis.

"The sun came first and the sun is an egg, of sorts," said Steve, "egg shaped-ish, and therefore feminine. A bringer of life."

"I don't know what you are talking about."

"Your Grandad has asked me to give you a father and son lesson. You have to bear with me. I'm building up to it."

The experiments in Steve Atherton's teenage years had begun with a channel of light in a pitch dark room. "The light, all light, is travelling at 670,615,200 miles a hour, but I can stop it in an instant, down to zero, by turning it off. See. Therefore I should be able to increase the speed by turning it up."

In time, he learned to push the light beyond its ordinary (he called it dormant) speed by energising it (he called it waking). The simplest method of energising or waking anything at atomic level was to heat it, but that caused changes in the atomic structure.

"Erm, Charlie. I think you should get your coat and join me in a run for home. The cave will confine the explosion, which is going to go, oh, in thirty to thirty three seconds time. On the upside, if we make it out alive, we will have a deeper cave."

"If we don't, we'll still have a deeper cave."

"Run!"

"And the baby grows in the womb, from the egg, the egg that has been fertilised. And that is called The Miracle of Life and it takes nine months. Nine. Any questions? No? Good. What? What have I said?"

The atomic compression method of squeezing atoms so that the electrons flew closer and therefore faster, to and around the nucleus, gave off a not unusable but quite impractical heat until Steve found the coolant, the stabiliser. Coloured light. The light had the surprising dual function of adding to the mass of the nucleus and therefore increasing it's gravity to give it an illogical but quite actual boost of speed. It was all so simple he was really quite surprised that no one had thought of it before. He found that the different colours in sunlight had different qualities and properties, particularly when 'mass' and 'weight' representing himself, Charlie and a spaceship, were factored into the experiments. Full light, or white light, was useless of course, it was too hot and quite incapable of moving solid matter. Yellow light could not be sufficiently energised to lift and carry anything heavier than dust. Red light was weaker still, but pure orange light was stronger than yellow but weaker than blue. This was because the chronology of rainbow colours shifted during atomic compression. Colours on the fringe were sometimes more effective than colours in the centre.

"It's as if God is hiding something. I said, 'it's as if God is hiding something'. If your eyes hadn't glazed over when I was explaining it all to you, which they did and don't try to deny it, then you would know that I'm on the very verge of the breakthrough. I'm almost there. I need to find two more things, the right colour and the right power source. I still need to find the secret ingredient of a regenerational self-perpetuating power source."

"Gravity," said Charlie.

"Gravity can only take you to the edge of light speed. Something else is needed to take you beyond it."

"The Sun," said Charlie.

"Yes, the Sun is the source but there's still something missing."

The secret to breaking all the known laws of physics were contained in the bruising of an eye. Charlie was ten-years-old when he bruised his eye in a game of rugby. A boy on the opposite team had grabbed the back of Charlie's shirt and used Charlie's own momentum to swing him to the ground. On the way round and down to the floor, Charlie's face had come into contact with the hip or the knee of another player. A boy on Charlie's own team in fact. The contact left Charlie with a bruised eye. The blue of his eye had filled with blood which temporarily coloured the eye purple. Blue plus Red equals Purple. Purple light proved to be the most practical and the most stable when compressed, when compressing, and also when carrying. "It's pretty obvious when you think it about it," said Steve. "Purple has always been associated with the Heavens, and it's pretty much in the middle of the bands red and blue."

"And gold," said Charlie. "Gold and silver."

"Yes. There will be secrets to Heaven contained in gold and silver. The entrance to Heaven will probably require a golden key. Now let me take another photograph of that eye of yours. The bruising has gone. I wonder if it has left behind another clue? You can see the whole world in a human eye."

"With an eye," said Charlie, as the light shone and the shutter closed.

"Yes," said Steve, "*with* an eye and *in* an eye. I was being poetic."

The clue to the power source had faded with the bruise, because that clue was in the making of the bruise. It was the bruise itself. The missing ingredient was blood. Human blood.

Chapter 22

The nights lengthened. The temperature rose. Summer came round again. And the scouts went camping. Charlie returned bronzed like an Australian and covered with scratches. "Look at your legs," said Steve. "They look as if the Crusaders have been trying to whip the skin from you."

"Oh, they're all right," said Charlie. "Look at this." He held out his right hand, the palm and wrist of which were patterned with raised red insect bites. "We built a treehouse in a bramble bush and slept there for two nights. On the last night, I was bitten by something called a Bastard."

Steve ran a finger across the swellings: "I wonder what it says?"

"What?"

"The swellings look like braille to me," said Steve. "I reckon the insect which bit you has left a message. You should shake hands with a blind man to find out what it says."

"I can read braille," said Charlie, easing a finger across the swellings. "It says, yum, yum, yum, yum, yum. All the way across."

"What about those two larger ones?"

"They say yum too, but with an exclamation mark."

Steve laughed.

"Insects don't have a big vocabularly."

"Do they itch?"

"Yes."

"Do you scratch them?"

"No. Anyway, I brought you this." He gave Steve a wood-carved owl, delightfully charming in its imperfections. "I carved it myself. Slim taught me how. Ask me what wood it is made from?"

"What wood is it?"

"Ash. Ask me what wood is used in this room?"

"Such as what?"

"That table."

"Okay. What's that table made from?"

"Walnut," said Charlie. "That cabinet-thing—"

"To give it its proper name."

"That cabinet thing is oak and the pattern carved on it is of a hawthorn bush."

"Bramble."

"Is it a bramble?"

"I think so."

"A hawthorn bramble. Slim taught me all about the properties of different woods, and we made a Roman wheel using a branch of steamed ash, heated at the side of the river, in a fire pit."

"He's a good man, Slim," said Steve. "He taught me how to swim, when I was eleven or twelve."

Charlie crinkled his brow and said: "Slim's older than you?"

"Older! he's twenty years older at least! He was *my* scout leader, you cheeky brat."

"I didn't know you were in the scouts?"

"Yes, you did. I've told you often enough."

Charlie moved the point of attack away from himself by saying, "You couldn't swim until you were twelve?"

"I could but I wasn't very good because I wasn't very confident in the water. Slim taught me how to dive in."

"From Grandad's jetty?"

"Yes, the jetty on Grandad's lake. Is it still there?"

"Yes."

"I remember spending whole summers on that lake when I was a boy."

"We didn't do much swimming this year."

"Looking back on it, Charlie, I think the day I learned to dive was the second most important day of my life."

"Why?"

"Because it turned a fear into a pleasure. That moment of conquest gave me the belief that I could do anything."

Chapter 23

A large explosion shook the windows in Grandma's house and caused the china plates to jump. One fell. Charlie caught it and said, "Ole!". He was disappointed no one was there to see him. He put the plate back in its proper place on the sideboard and he ran outside. The explosion was big enough to send not just Charlie but Grandad and Grandma running over to where it came from, Steve's house. Grandma, who was in the front garden at the time of the explosion, led the race, her hands gripping tighter on a pair of pruning scissors. Charlie brought up the rear, holding back, and strangely relaxed. Dogs were barking from behind garden gates; an irritated burglar alarm screamed and screamed and screamed and stopped. Neighbours were in the street. Officers Adams and Alva radioed in for help. There was a general air of concern.

Charlie looked up. It was a lovely sunny day.

From the back of the house, Steve emerged, hands raised as if trying to surrender. "Sorry, everyone. Sorry about that. Just a little experiment. That's all. Sorry." The neighbours crowded him, concerned but glad to have the opportunity to intrude. All relief and overdone smiles. Charlie stepped back from the crowd after catching Steve's eye. He sat down on the kerb. The look, imperceptible to anyone else, said: "I've done it! I've built a forcefield which works!"

One by one, then two by two, the neighbours, the policemen, and the late arriving squad cars and ambulances went away until there was only Steve, Grandma, Grandad and Charlie Ellis. Distant church bells rang in the hour. Grandad, fitter and more healthy this week than last, said to Steve: "I won't press you for any details, but..." He patted Charlie on the head and said: "If you don't mind, I'll leave this little fellow with you in the hope it keeps you from further mischief."

Grandma kissed Steve on the cheek. Charlie got to his feet.

"It's good news I take it?" said Grandad.

"It's very good news," said Steve.

"Well, you two will have a lot to talk about then."

"What time should I come back, Grandad?"

"We'll have dinner at eight, Charlie. Eight. Eight-thirty? Will that give you enough time?"

"Yes," said Steve.

"Good. Since this is a special day, we'll cook something special. Bring Charlie back at eight o'clock. You'll join us, of course?"

"Thank you," said Steve.

Grandad and Grandma went home.

Steve smiled. And Charlie smiled.

For a long time, they stood at the roadside without talking.

Chapter 24

The foundry, known locally as The Bronze Fort, on account of its high walls and its massive and intricately carved bronze doorway, was reached by a footpath curling from the lower hill entrance of the Bat Cave, to the left of the lake known as The Pond. On the mid-morning walk over, Steve pointed out a bird's nest.

"Do you see that parcel of trees over there?"

"Parcel of trees?"

"Yes."

"*Parcel* of *trees*?" said Charlie incredulously.

"That's what it's called, a parcel of trees, a perfectly good collective noun."

"Of *trees*?"

"A gift for your grammar. Do you see the nest?"

"So that's where the cameras are?"

"No," said Steve. "That's a bird's nest. I was seeing if you knew which one?"

"Chaffinch," guessed Charlie, confidently but not correctly.

"Is it?" asked Steve, surprised and disappointed that Charlie might know. He thought, 'I've been neglecting his and my own education, too self-focused on my experiments.' Then he said: "I'd say it was more likely to be an owl."

"This close to the lake?"

Steve wondered if there was any relevance between owls, lakes and the optimum distance between them. He knew that an owl's diet was more mouse-based than fish-based, and he knew too that Charlie had him in check with a checkmate looming, so he changed the subject. "What did you do in Bristol yesterday?"

"You know what I did in Bristol."

"Oh, the art exhibition. Was it good?"

"It was Edvard Munch."

"I like Munch."

"I know. I was surprised you didn't want to see it."

"It's not that I didn't want to. It's just that I'm so busy."

With a wry pomposity, Charlie impersonated Steve's voice and walk and repeated something Steve had said to him: "A wise man is never so busy as to let the world go by."

"You are becoming insufferable," said Steve, pleasantly. He tried to rub Charlie's head, but Charlie ducked away and laughed.

"Grandad said people have a duty to immerse themselves in the *Atmospheric Saturation of Beauty*."

"That's a good phrase," said Steve.

"That's what he said going into gallery."

"There's not much beauty in Munch, a few sun on water landscapes, perhaps."

"He didn't like it. He didn't like the exhibition. He bought you a picture though."

"Did he?"

"For Christmas. They were selling these cloth ones of the sun. He bought you one of those for Christmas. It's a secret."

The foundry had been built in the last quarter of the nineteenth century to cast industrial components; mostly iron girders used in the construction of railway bridges. A red-brick chimney towered above the forest trees. In recent years, the foundry had diversified to accommodate the indulgent follies of Brit Art, giant pop art statues in aluminum, bronze and steel. The diversification had been made possible by an investment grant from the foundry's current owner, Charlie's Grandad, and by the secret commissions for Spaceship One and now Spaceship Two. The grant had been so generous that it guaranteed the lifelong prosperity of everyone who worked at the foundry but was tied to the condition of secrecy. All employees signed loyalty contracts so binding that, even if they turned tail and sold their stories to the government or to the press, the legal ramifications would be ruinous for them, not that it would ever come to that. The work-life-balance contract earned by all employees at the foundry was so harmonious it would put the most generous continental equivalents to shame. People arrived at work happy, and they left with smiles on their faces. Grandad liked to say, and perhaps it was true, that he took his business model from the *Snow White* film by Walt Disney. Seeing the film at an impressionable age had a lasting effect on him. "Men and women should go to work singing, and whistle while they work. Now what I can give them to put the smiles back on their faces?"

"Mr. Atherton, Sir. It's a good morning for it." The guard opened the first outer door to the first inner courtyard. Steve liked coming here. The workers treated him with the nodding respect grown up children reserve for old favoured teachers. "I would like to have watched the demonstration, but someone has to hold the fort."

"They do. Yes," replied Steve. "I appreciate it."

"Thank you, Sir." The guard nodded his repect and led Steve and

Charlie through a short tunnelled maze that led to the second outer door, if you went the right way. The guard opened and closed the door behind Steve and Charlie, then returned to his post, whistling.

"How are you feeling, Charlie?"

"Good."

"Nervous?"

"Yes, a bit."

On the factory floor, Steve shook hands with Bill Butler, the foreman, an impressively stout man in a hard hat and black and green overalls. On the gantries all around, a watching workforce waited. After a brief conversation, Bill gave the signal and moved away from Steve in the centre of the courtyard and took his place on a raised platform holding The Main Man, as the workers called him, Charlie's Grandad.

"Have you seen him do his tricks yet?" Grandad asked of Bill.

"I never thought I'd see a forcefield," said Bill.

On a nod from Grandad, Steve activated a forcefield from a small cube held in his hands. When he pressed the cube, something almost invisible surrounded him. You could see Steve clearly, but the light seemed to bend around him. There was a hint of blue. Grandad called a halt to the experiment by standing up and waving at Steve. Steve turned off the forcefield.

"We can see you?" said Grandad.

"I've programmed it to let light through."

"Doesn't that compromise it?"

"It's safe," said Steve.

But what did that mean? It's *safe*? If Grandad had thought the answer through instead of sitting back down and giving the signal to start again, he would have realised that it meant, 'Yes, I have weakened the forcefield. It is no longer strong enough to hold back light.' But that didn't mean that the forcefield was useless.

Steve turned the forcefield back on. A worker walked towards him wearing an iron mask and carrying a flame-thrower, green and black. Flames dripped from the nozzle like saliva from a hungry dragon's mouth. The worker pointed the nozzle at Steve, pulled a leaver towards himself, and flame rushed forth with a roar that was as thrilling as it was fearsome. The flame coloured the whole courtyard orange and warmed the faces of the workers. It even made their mouths drop open with disbelief. But it did nothing at all to the forcefield.

The second, third and fourth tests were much more impressive. For the Second Test, Steve Atherton stood inside a twenty feet by twenty feet concrete bowl. Above him tilted a tubular container that released a cascade of molten iron, now rolling red-yellow-white down the outside of the forcefield like an infernal shower. The liquid iron collected underneath Steve, lifting him up, so that he and the forcefield floated. Not anticipating this oceanic roll, Steve fell over, causing liquid metal to splash over the walls of the tank. Everyone was sufficiently far away for this not to be a problem but, in the wait for Test Three, he spent ten busy minutes apologising: "I'm sorry. I'm really very sorry about that."

It could have been a disaster.

Test Three brought a very British response from the watching workforce, who winced and gasped without melodramatics as a nine-ton cast-iron drum was dropped forty-five feet, from a crane, onto Steve Atherton's head. "Like raindrops on an umbrella," he said, stepping unhurt and untroubled around the dropped drum, and feeling very much like a character in a Chuck Jones cartoon.

Test Four took the longest to prepare but failed to run its course. Steve sat inside a furnace. The door was closed and the furnace fired. The intention was for him to stay inside for ten minutes, but Charlie got so anxious and agitated that the experiment was cut short. The door to the furnace was opened and Steve was coaxed out.

"I didn't like it, Steve."

With great discretion, he wiped away the boy's tears.

Chapter 25

Charlie's tears at the testing session moved Steve more in retrospect than they did at the time for they woke the demon of the angel called Conscience. It rose from a pit in his stomach and it settled at the back of his mind. And it wouldn't let go. Was it right for him, Steve Atherton, to endanger a boy whose life experience was insufficient for him to truly understand the dangers of the impressive itinery ahead? Was it right to endanger one who was too young to understand the importance of Life itself? Like the patriotic and foolhardy boy soldiers who, from the beginning of time, have taken up arms in support of a cause they hold to be more important than themselves, he knew that Charlie wouldn't shy away from a mission that could mean Death. But was it right for Steve Atherton to allow Charlie Ellis that choice? Would it be right to awaken the boy's consciousness by talking to him about the dangers? Was ignorance bliss? How much did Charlie Ellis really know?

And what about the blood? Will these wounds ever heal? He rubbed the itching wounds on the underside of his arms.

As the construction of Spaceship Two progressed, Steve found himself distancing himself from Charlie. He didn't welcome him as warmly when he arrived at the Bat Cave. He asked him to leave at an earlier hour than had become their norm. He didn't take him on the six-day trip to America.

"But you said it wasn't useful?" said Charlie.

"It wasn't. They talk but they don't listen."

"So, why are you going back?"

"Because I have to."

"That's not an answer," said Charlie.

Steve sighed: "I saw a child crushed in the crowd that greeted me at the airport. I'm going back to see the child and to apologise."

"It wasn't your fault," said Charlie.

"It was," said Steve.

The effect of this mood change of Steve's was to jump start adolescent introspection in Charlie Ellis. He became quieter, more watchful, more thoughtful, less useful, less fun. This, in turn, brought Grandad's spirits down so low that, in time, Grandad found he lacked the energy to rise from his morning bed. With her husband of almost fifty years now talking of going to the land of the dead, Grandma did as all good Grandmas do. She treated the symptoms and she tackled the cause. Her meeting with Steve, gentle at first, over tea in her house, increased in passion and pace over the common ground of the village green, to continue in Steve's house, in his ear, in his face. It ended hours later with whispered apologies and a warm embrace.

"Charlie, my love." Her weight now upon the boy's bed.

"What is it Gran? I heard you shouting at Steve. What's going on?"

"He's a lovely man, Charlie. You know that. And he loves you very much, and you know that too. He's sorry for the way he's been acting recently, and he'll apologise to you himself I'm sure. He's had a lot on his mind, you see. And it had been getting him down. He'll be better soon. He's getting over it. He's sorry. Tomorrow we're all going swimming, first thing."

"Swimming?"

"Yes, all of us. At the lake."

"I didn't know you could swim?"

"Swim! Where do you think I met your Grandfather? There weren't discos in my day."

"Is Grandad going to get better?" asked Charlie.

"Of course he'll get better. He'll be up like a shot in the morning. Just mark my words."

And he was. And he did. And the day, long, was good.

Chapter 26

It truly was a wonder to behold. The forest road was closed to get it there. In the hour before dawn, workmen moved into position with heavy machinery. They dug up the road at points East and West to close it to all unauthorised traffic. The forest was scanned and cleared by a line of beaters and huntsman. On completing their sweep, with dawn inching in, the signal was given for the foundry gates to be opened. Workers gasped as the hydraulic sections of the forest parted, folding away to let the wide-load lorries through.

Hidden beneath a roped tarpaulin, black and green, the cargo was hoisted onto the take-off platform. When the ropes were removed, the platform withdrew, taking the cargo into the hillside. The hillside closed. The workers left. The forest returned to a perfect imitation of nature, helped along by lines of men in Grandad's employ. Steamrollers flattened down newly laid tarmac. The day's first cars motored by, unaware that an engineering marvel had taken place. Now, with the tarpaulin cloth pulled away like a curtain, the cargo gleamed pearl white beneath a toothy ceiling and before a smiling boy. "It's beautiful! It's beautiful Steve!"

At more than four times the size of the original spaceship, and with a design close to perfection, it was so impressive it made Spaceship One look like the work of amateurs. Charlie ran beneath the track on which it lay, his hand sliding smooth across the bodywork. The solar cells in the white metal winked.

Grandad popped open a bottle of champagne which spilled in bubbled applause. "To the future," he said.

"To us all," said Grandma.

"To my great friends," said Steve, raising his glass. "And to The Seagull".

"The Seagull?"

"That's what I wanted to call the spaceship, after the bird who dared."

"Charlie won't like that," said Grandma.

"He didn't," said Steve.

They laughed and raised their glasses, and they drank to The Seagull, its name if only for that moment of dedication, with Charlie lost in a cheek-to-metal caress.

Chapter 27

It didn't take long for Steve to install and fine-tune the engines. "They're silent but if you listen closely you can hear the singing of wolves."

"No, you can't," said Charlie.

"Yes, you can. Where should we start? West to East, or East to West?"

"What?" asked Charlie.

"It's logical to follow a circular path. So, do we set off Eastwards or do we fly out West?"

"Does it matter?"

"Yes," said Steve.

"Why?"

"Look at the maps and tell me."

Charlie looked at the maps and did a few sums. "West to East," he said. "We'll save about, well - I can't do the necessary calculations, because I don't know all the orbital times, but it is quicker going West to East."

"That may be true," said Steve, "but I can think of at least three pressing reasons why we have to go East to West."

"What are they?"

"You tell me."

Charlie looked at the data before him and said: "Give me a clue."

"What wrecked our last trip?"

"I don't think it did, but I presume you mean the meteorite?"

"Yes."

"And that's the clue?"

"Yes."

Charlie looked at the star maps again, his fingers sliding between the planets. "There's a meteorite field between Mars and Jupiter. I'm guessing, but will the field be thinner if we go East to West?"

"It will be. Good lad. That's one point. What else?"

Charlie gave it some thought and said: "Is it a trick question?"

"A bit of *solve et coagule.*"

"Is the answer reasonable and scientific or is it *poetic*?"

"Clever boy. Now you're really starting to use your brain."

"So it's poetic?"

Steve shrugged his shoulders.

"East to West. The planets move from East to West?"

"Mostly, yes. I'll give you that. Point two. Think of your history."

"In history," said Charlie, "people have always moved to the West from the East; from East Europe to West Europe. From Europe to America. And, as Grandad says, 'from Australia to Bloody Everywhere.'"

"Don't swear."

"That wasn't swearing."

"It was. Don't do it. Do you give up?"

"Give me a clue?"

"The sun rises in the East."

"And sets in the West," said Charlie.

"Yes. We're quite a team."

"We should be on television?"

"We're always on television," said Steve.

The sequence was concluded thus: when Spaceship Two was operational, tested, and approved, they would go to Jupiter first, then to Saturn, Pluto, Uranus, Neptune, Venus and Mercury. They aimed to arrive at Mercury in May.

Chapter 28

Charlie was tearing up pages from his work book, calculations done, problems solved and answers memorized: "Is the navigation programming done? It'll take me ages to check it all, and you said not to start it until I've got it all in front of me?"

"The computers are still working through the Atherton scans. I don't want there to be any surprises. I'm going to the shops tomorrow. What do you want for your birthday?"

"What?"

"We'll be away on your birthday, so I'll have to get you something before we go."

"A robot," said Charlie.

"I was thinking along the lines of a book or some music, some Elvis?"

"C3PO."

"What?"

"A robot like C3PO. Something that's useful."

"C3PO isn't useful."

"He can speak every known language in the universe," said Charlie. "Very useful if we get lucky."

"C3PO is an actor who speaks English and probably a bit of half-remembered school French."

"Which is why we need a robot *like* C3PO," said Charlie.

"For your birthday?"

"Yes."

Steve leant back in his chair, his hands behind his head. He was quiet for a while. Then he said: "R2D2 would be easier; a simpler design, more obvious uses."

"Such as?"

"I could fit him with attachments so he could link into the ship's computer and run tests."

"A detached back-up computer?"

"Yes."

"Is that safe?"

"No. We'd still need an integrated back-up."

"So it's a waste of space. The robot you've agreed to make me will have to be useful to justify its passage."

"I didn't agree to make one."

"You did."

"When?"

"Just now," said Charlie grinning. "I know you're getting old, but I hope you're not losing your memory?"

Steve rubbed Charlie's head in such a way that said 'You are a cheeky monkey'. "I'll make you a robot. But I can only spend a few weeks on it, and tweak it here and there when we're on board, and you're in bed."

"What?"

"You'll have to wait until your birthday before you see it, otherwise it won't be a surprise."

"Oh."

"And it won't look like C3PO because there's a copyright on the design. And you do know that robotics isn't my thing?"

"I know."

"So the robot may not be any good."

"I know," said Charlie, grinning rudely.

Chapter 29

The first test flight of Spaceship Two, waved off by Charlie and his grandparents, had been a failure. There was something wrong with the ballast, which made manual steering difficult; and the forcefield rendered the projection screens useless, so there was no view of the outside from the inside of the ship. This put the project back more than two months until Steve and Charlie worked out and applied the solutions.

The second test flight, this time with Steve and Charlie on board, was successful but for a slowness in the interchanging of the interiors. To fix this, the engineers had to rebuild a section of the interior, and this took them a few days short of a month.

With the spaceship now handling well, Charlie began his solo flight lessons, all begun in early morning darkness, but he made the mistake of helping himself to one when Steve wasn't in the Bat Cave to supervise. Charlie was in outer space when the screen came on. It was Grandma. She didn't look angry, but she didn't look happy. With a deceptive calmness, she said: "Charlie, what are you doing?"

"I'm in outer space, Gran."

"I can see you're in outer space. I asked what are you doing?"

"Just—"

"Just coming back home," said Grandma. "I don't want you flying on your own."

"Steve said —."

"Steve had no right to give you permission, and I'll tell him as much when he gets back from London. What time does he get back?"

"Not until tomorrow."

"Grandad wants to talk to you. He's very upset."

"Upset? Why?"

"Because of your stealing."

"I didn't steal anything."

"And because of your lying."

"Lying?"

"About the stealing."

"Oh, you mean the *pie*?"

"And the bread, and the cheese."

"I forgot the brandy."

"*Brandy!*"

"It was a literary theft, Gran. I took it as a sign."

"You're not making any sense, Charlie Ellis."

"I left a note in my room explaining everything, Gran. It's from *Great Expectations*. You said I could make a packed lunch."

"A packed lunch portion."

"Pip, in *Great Expectations*, steals a pork pie, some bread, a curd of cheese, and some brandy to give to an escaped convict. When I saw the pork pie and the cheese curd in the larder, I took it as a sign that I should Go To London, so to speak."

"Go to London?"

"And become a gentleman. And learn how to box. You know?"

'I don't know. But I do know you are nowhere near London."

'I don't mean *go to London* literally. I'm talking literarely. But I forgot to take the brandy. You only had sherry and I didn't know if that was the same."

"Charlie Ellis!"

"I'm going to bring it back."

"Well you're not making sense to me. I'll talk clearly to make sure you understand me. Are you listening?"

"I'm listening, Gran."

"Bring the spaceship back home, right now, or I'll press the button."

"Button?"

"The Tractor Beam button on the remote control."

"There isn't a Tractor Beam button?"

"It says Tractor Beam quite clearly. And it also says it returns the ship to base and renders it useless."

"Where are you? The Bat Cave?"

"No, I'm in the sitting room," said Gran.

Could Steve have rigged up a Tractor Beam to pull the spaceship back home? And could it really have been programmed into Grandma's remote control? Charlie didn't think it was possible. He'd already resolved to turn the ship round and come back home, but he inadvertantly annoyed Gran by erroneously repeating: "But there isn't a Tractor Beam button?"

She pressed the button with more push than was really necessary, and with a temper that turned off the viewing screen with an audible pop. "Woooahhh!" said Charlie, as the controls were taken away from him and away from the ship's computer. He fell down with the swooping and the dropping of the ship.

"Damn," he said to himself.

The screen came on again. It was Grandma.

"And I don't want to hear any more of that swearing, Charlie Ellis."

"That wasn't swearing," said Charlie.

"And no back chat. And you can answer to your Grandfather when you get in."

The upshot of this was that the SUP Mission was cancelled.

"Finished for today, for tomorrow, forever. Amen. I won't change my mind," said Charlie's grandmother. And she meant it. But Grandad talked her out of it. 'The things I do for science,' he said to himself. In return, he really thought that Steve should hand over the Nobel Prize to him as a thank you. Share it with him at the very least. 'He does the maths and the doing, I suppose, but he would get nowhere without me,' so thought Charlie's Grandad. 'If Mr. Atherton were an honorable man, and I think he is, he would share it with me gladly. I won't ask him to because that would be rude of me, a good man should be allowed to give without the old heave-ho. But I think I might start dropping some hints. Let's see how it pans out. Yes, a Nobel Prize. I like the sound of that. I wonder if it adds some letters to my name?'.

Chapter 30

Charlie's solo flight wasn't the only time he and Steve got into trouble in the run-up to the SUP Mission. They were both feeling low and run down when they sat down to write the letters of apology for a greater failing of trust that befell them after the inauguration flight later that month. Neither Steve nor Charlie could remember whose idea it had been to invite the scouts. Steve wanted to take the blame but Charlie wouldn't let him.

"It's my fault, Steve. You're not even a member."

The discussion continued in circles before playing out in a stalemate of half-sulks and rude silences. Steve started it up again by saying: "Well, it's a sign that you're growing up."

"What is?"

"Knowing that one should take responsibility for one's actions. That's what this is all about; and that's why, in the perverse way of bureaucrats, they were right, to some degree, to do what they did."

"No they weren't. I can't believe you just said that," said Charlie.

"I don't agree with what they did. But I do understand that to them, in their way of thinking, they were right to do what they did."

"No they weren't!"

"It's all about taking responsibility for one's actions."

"I know. And it was my fault. So I've got to take the blame. They can sack me from the scouts. *I don't care.*"

"It wasn't your fault, Charlie. I'm responsible for you. I'm responsible for everything you do."

"No you're not."

"And Slim was responsible for the scouts. Don't you see that?"

"Yes, but it was my idea."

"I don't think it was your idea, Charlie. And I don't want this to go round in circles again. I know you're not going to let me take the blame, and you must know that I'm not going to let you take the blame and, though you've turned down the offer already, I think the only way forward is to write the letters together."

Charlie sighed and was silent. Then with gentle resignation, he said: "All right, but they must be in my handwriting. You can sign them as well if you want to."

It had been a difficult few weeks. Steve or Charlie had made the suggestion to invite the scouts on board for The Inauguration Flight. Slim himself was enthusiastic. The scouts were ecstatic. Parental permission slips had been printed and distributed and that is when the problems started. Most parents were thrilled by the rare opportunity for their sons, but some objected on the grounds that it was too dangerous. One parent tried to insist on trying it first himself (declined), and one parent declared that it too dangerous not only for her son but for everyone's son. With the zeal of loveless bigot, or a bored British bureaucrat given a rush by a brush with fame, she pursued her complaint through all the proper channels and sold the story to one of the cheaper newspapers. Cheap newspapers move quickly but proper channels move slowly, and time was short. The SUP project was already three months behind schedule; further rescheduling would mean a complete rewriting of the navigation programmes so, when the trouble with the parent flared, and the press men came snooping, cameras flashgunning Grandad asleep in a worn deckchair, Steve withdrew the offer of the spaceflight for the scouts. There were many upset boys and many angry and thoughtless words directed at Charlie. Slim intervened but the damage had been done. Friendships had been lost.

Later that week, Slim arrived at Steve's house and, from there, probably at Slim's suggestion, the plan was hatched to carry out the flight in secret. The parents of the boys who supported the trip were visited and given the new arrangements. Behind the cover of a Saturday morning hike, the invited boys were to meet at the Scout Hut and walk together to the take-off spot near the trig point on Horsepool Hill. But this did not go according to plan. On seeing the spaceship arrive, one of the boys had a panic attack and couldn't be coaxed on board. Slim contacted the boy's parents and was told they would be right along, but the parents settled instead on doing a few small chores. When the chore-happy parents arrived almost fifty minutes later, the spaceship had gone. To avoid parental censure, their son, feeling empty and foolish, feigned distress. Slim had offered to stay with the stay-behind boy but Steve had reminded him of his obligation to the boys already on board ("And I'm not prepared to handle this lot by myself"). The boy's parents, enraged to the point of vindictiveness, were pushed by a tabloid paper to sue for compensation. It was beyond them to understand that the presence of a spaceship on a public hill had attracted a busy crowd of on-lookers and one very loud and very rude press man.

"We could blast him by turning on the forcefield," said Charlie.

"No, we can't," said Steve.

"But he's banging on the side. Won't he damage it?"

"No," said Steve.

"Does the electrocution thing not work?"

"Not on this ship, Charlie. But it is time to get going. Okay lads. We're going to take off." There was a lot of cheering.

The original plan, for the first part of the trip, had been to film a variation of the start of the famous film, *Powers of Ten* by Ray and Charles Eames. Steve and Charlie both had seen the Eames film at school, more than twenty years apart. It had fired their imagination. In the film, the camera starts on a fixed point one metre above the Earth, above a couple relaxing after picnicking at a Lake near Chicago. The camera then rises at a continuously increasing pace so that after every ten seconds it has risen ten times higher to a view that is ten times larger. It travels upwards through all known space, past all the planets and, on reaching the extent of Man's Knowledge in 1977, it travels back and descends into the sleeping man's body, right through his layers of skin, right down to atomic level.

Steve and Charlie's plan had been to take the spaceship up to one hundred thousand miles, all the while filming the view from the reference marker on the crown of the hill (the Scout Hut being obscured from above by trees). But this was England. The cloud cover prevented it. Almost nothing could be seen. And, in fact, the camera didn't start recording at the right moment or from the right position. To shield the scouts from the sight on Horsepool Hill of the nutter banging on the side of the spaceship, Steve had turned the viewing screens off and kept them off. In his fluster, and not having any visuals to guide him, he miscalcuated the distance for the horizontal drift to the trig point by more than a hundred feet, so the symmetry of the image was missed. The *Powers of Ten* tribute film was abandoned when Steve saw one of the boys pressing a button on a control panel on the wall. The spaceship was hovering at fifty thousand feet. Steve said: "I'm sorry, I don't know your name."

"Robert."

"Robert, please don't touch that. Remember, you have given your word of honour to look and not to touch. There is no chance of you doing any harm by pressing those buttons, because I spent much of last night re-programming the controls to respond only to the fingertips of the full-time crew, but I'm holding you at your honour. Is that understood?"

"Yes, Sir."

"All of you?"

"Yes, Sir."

"Thank you, but there's no need to call me Sir. I'm Steve Atherton. You can call me Steve, or you can call me Mr. Atherton, whichever you're most comfortable with. Some of you older ones will remember me, from a while back, when I came to the Hut to try to get you interested in Science. I gave out a few badges and I gave a talk. Can any of you remember what the talk was about?"

A dark-haired boy put up his hand and said: "You showed us a film about the moon."

"Yes, that's right."

Another boy interrupted: "You'd made a robot thing that flew to the moon and which made that film."

"Yes, I'd made a flying film camera which crashed into the moon, unfortunately, because I'd miscalculated the strength of the gravitational pull but, before it crashed, the camera managed to send back the film I showed you."

Questions were asked and prompted and answered. Then Steve said: "Well, I've given you enough clues. Can any of you guess where we're going today?" The boys were cheering and jumping for joy before Steve could nod and say 'yes'.

"Screens on," said Steve. The ship's interior flooded with clean sunlight. There were gasps of amazement. "We're hovering at fifty thousand feet. The cloud layer beneath us means that we can't see the ground, but you'll be able to see it as we ease our way out of the Earth's atmosphere. One of my favourite things about space travel is the moment when you break from a blue sky into an all black sky. We'll go slowly so you can savour the transformation."

It was hugely impressive.

"Now, the purpose of the trip is to do three complete loops of the moon. It is exciting to see the moon up close, we'll go slowly around it so you can all have a good look, and you can all take photographs. Pay special attention when we go round what is called the dark side of the moon. We can only see one side of the moon from Earth, so you'll be among the very few people in history who have seen the dark side. When we've done one complete loop, we'll do a two more using the co-ordinates of the famous slingshot manoeuver. Do any of you know what that is?" The boys all knew what it was. "That's right. In the early days of manned spaceflight, a brilliantly brave team of Americans had to loop round the moon and use the trajectory as a slingshot to get themselves home. So we'll follow that trajectory in honour of them. That trajectory, or slingshot, will send us towards the Pacific Ocean of course, so we'll have a nice flight back across the Ocean, and across Ireland before we get home. When you write your reports of this day, and I hope you all write up this day if only for your children, and their children's children, it will improve your report if you can put it into the context of the adventurers who have gone before you. The journey we are about to make will be written about and talked about for as long as there are people who can write and who can talk. You are all adventurers now."

He raised his head to the computer banks and said: "To the moon, please. Two hours."

Two hours was the time he'd estimated for the boys' hearts to steady down to a level from which the surge of the new emotion would be best enjoyed. Currently the boys were all cheering. Then, with the cheers of boys still ringing in his ears, pushed along by one intensely happy lad who was still cheering when all the others had stopped, he said to himself: 'What have I become? Once a pure scientist, now a showman shouting, Roll up! Roll up! Ah well, it's only for a day. Then Conscience kicked in and asked 'Is it? Is it only for a day, Steve? What are you doing out here? You and the boy? You're just showing off. That's all you ever do. That's all you've ever done'. Then Common Sense arrived, carried in on the backs of the smiles on the scout troop's faces. Common Sense told him to stop being so hard on himself.

He looked at Charlie, his young face masked behind a hard serious expression. Charlie was showing the boys who didn't have cameras how to take photographs using the ship's interior and exterior hardware. He had about him the air of a natural born teacher. His mother would have been so proud of him.

Then Steve looked at Slim, dear old kind old Slim, thrilled to be up here, for sure, but his full attention taken by a runt of a lad with an upturned nose. He watched as Slim addressed the boy's problem and then worked the room, missing nothing and no one.

This group of happy children was by no means an unrepresenta-tive selection of the male youth of England. There were average boys and energetic boys, nervous boys and noisy boys, there were two sensitive-looking lads whose slightly distant airs suggested dreams of a higher life.

Then a small boy was asking Steve a question. Steve answered him as simply and as clearly as he could, but he saw the boy's eyes glaze over and he knew he hadn't gotten through. He thought, 'Why can't all boys be like Charlie? Why are some boys stupid?'. Chiding him-self for this pomposity, he resolved to learn from Slim's example. He worked the room, listening, prompting, answering. He posed for photographs, signed Scout record books and, through the viewing screens, he directed wide-open eyes to points of rare and worthy interest. He was only just hitting his stride when the moon come up so close that it filled the main viewing screen. At first, and for a considerable time, there was only the held breath of boy-silence.

"Okay, we'll hold it here. We'll park here for a while. It's a good place to draw pictures and to take photographs. Can you see those ridges? They're the mountains on the moon. We'll stay here for a while, and then we'll go in close and have a look at those mountains, and then we'll do the loops around."

When the drawings had been done and the photographs all taken, Steve told everyone to put their books away and, when that was done, to give Slim their attention. "And silence, please." The boys gave Slim their attention.

"Thank you. Now we have reached the main moment of the trip. The highlight of the trip. The real reason for the trip. In a couple of minutes time you are going to see a sight so wonderful that your spirits will strengthen so completely that they can never be broken. I want you to think deeply about the thing that you are about to see. Keep it always in your hearts. And never ever ever let it down."

The room was so silent you could only here the gentle wheezing of an asthmatic boy called Peter. Slim's ears had long been tuned to monitor the changes in its pitch.

Steve took hold of the ship's controls and switched the settings to manual. Checking data to the left and to the right of him, mostly concerning the positioning of the sun, he took the spaceship closer to the mountains of the moon, then he took the spaceship slowly over the curvature of the moon's horizon. There were gasps of amazement when they looped over and down and saw the single most impressive sight in the whole universe - the planet Earth.

The journey back to Earth took longer than two hours, necessarily so, to allow the boys pause to preserve their thoughts and to prepare themselves mentally for a life on Earth that had been coloured by a vision of its paradisal beauty.

Back at Horsepool Hill, after the patrol leaders led the customary communal shouts and thanks, and before the scouts departed together to walk the wooded route back to the Hut and to their waiting parents, Slim shook Steve's hand, left hand in left, and said: "Thank you, Steve. It's been a good day."

"It's been great, Slim."

"The boys will remember it forever."

Two week's later, it didn't bring Slim any comfort that his troop's adventure was the cover feature of a special edition of the world magazine of Boy Scouting for, by then, the bureaucrats had had their day and he had been suspended from running the troop. At a disciplinary hearing later, he was found guilty of neglecting a child in his care and of endangering the lives of boys in his protection. Incredibly, he was sacked from the Scout Movement. The sacking could be overturned on appeal, and his cause was championed by a tabloid rival to the one that had paid to condemn him, but Slim was too principled, and inwardly too distressed, to complain. So Charlie and Steve's letters were never officially answered.

Slim lived out his life in the village of his birth, and he never worked with boy scouts again.

Chapter 31

News of the scouts' journey to the moon brought an upsurge of visitors to Roeminster. The SUP mission had not been officially announced, nor had the launch point been indicated, but rumour was rife and a consensus soon formed. People came to Horsepool Hill in such numbers that Steve and Charlie felt duty bound, after pressure from Grandad, to not disappoint them. The media, fearing it had been caught cold, sacked executives for failing to secure the rights, although no broadcast rights had been offered nor any press conference called. Steve and Charlie had no intention of offering unedited transmissions of the journey. Instead, they planned to edit the footage themselves and to offer only the edited film. It would be released in Imax cinemas first because it was being filmed with Imax cameras.

"But, Steve, what about the people who can't afford to go the cinema? Some of Grandma's friends can't. Miss Bryanston is poor."

"We'll insist on free showings for pensioners and the poor."

"Pensioners Tuesday, or something?" said Charlie.

"And Low Wage Wednesday," said Steve. "And free showings for soldiers and the police."

"And firemen," said Charlie. "And-".

"There won't be anyone left to buy a ticket."

"There'll only be Grandad."

"He's a pensioner," said Steve.

"Oh, yes."

"But we've got to make the film before we can write our conditions in the contracts. Have you read the instruction book for operating the cameras? The three cameras are slightly different and there is a box of spares. Do you know how to load a magazine?"

Charlie nodded. "Cedric gave me a lesson. Oh, Grandad told me to tell you that the police are worried by the crowds on Horsepool Hill, and he wants to know when do you think we'll be ready?"

"How soon do you want it to be?"

"When do you want me to be ready for?"

"It's up to you, Charlie Ellis."

Charlie shrugged his shoulders and said: "Soon."

They shook hands.

Charlie was surprised his heart was beating faster than it should be.

Grandma oversaw the food, the oxygen, the water, the cleaning products, clothes and other supplies but it was Grandad who talked about how exhausting it all was, and how he was looking forward to "finally getting some peace". He'd spent the morning inspecting the books in Steve and Charlie's library, most of which he had put there. At lunchtime, he took away a book of poems by Philip Larkin that he had long meant to read himself. In return, he brought back a treasured edition of Byron's *Childe Harold*, signed by the author to the publisher. He was delighted by how good it looked on the shelf in the spaceship. He gave it pride of place. Then he decided against giving it away so he took the Byron back with him when he went home for a mid-afternoon nap. "There's no point in running myself into the ground."

The nap gave him the good idea to return to the Bat Cave with a paperback edition of Byron's *Childe Harold*. He'd reasoned that the annotations in the paperback edition were worth having, particularly if Charlie and Steve were not well read in the literature and politics of the period. But he didn't have a paperback copy, so he drove to Roeminster to buy one, but the traffic was too busy so, to keep his temper at bay, he turned the car around and drove to Gloucester. He had always said that he is not allowed to go to Gloucester without visiting his club so, after buying a paperback copy of the Byron, he went for a quick hello to the club, and stayed on for dinner because to not stay "would be a waste". Then he had to wait an hour after dinner because he'd had a glass of wine with his food. Back at The Bat Cave, he wrote a note and tucked it into the book, and he spent some time finding the right place on the right shelf for the book. The note said: 'Charlie, this is a good-bad book by a good-bad man. Admire him by his reach. Don't judge him by his failings.'

That night he fell asleep to the sound of his wife cleaning her teeth. His last words before sleeping were: "I've been working like a Polish salt miner. Another day like that will finish me off."

PART THREE

THE SEVEN
UNCONQUERED PLANETS

Grandad was in a bad mood. He had been in a bad mood for weeks as the upsurge in visitors to the town slowed down his day, and happy crowds blocked the pathways and added weight and numbers to the queues and services. It was now almost impossible to take a car into town. The streets were too full of tourist traffic. He was thinking of getting a passport barrier installed. He thought of getting his man on the council to print up signs saying 'These shops are for local people', but he knew he wouldn't do that. He was furious that a market trader was selling T-shirts with Charlie Ellis's face on them, and was annoyed that the trader mistook his complaint of "That's my grandson!" for a boast, and was rewarded with a hug and the attentions of an adoring crowd called forth by the market trader. He was annoyed by the way the crowd lifted their camera phones like crosses in a me-me-me perversion of the Catholic mass as they captured and shared their enfabling icons of Me and Now. "Get out of my way! Move away! I haven't got time for this."

Grandma didn't understand what he was talking about when he tried to explain what he meant about the perversion of The Mass but she knew what he meant when he said, "I told them to 'bugger off'."

"I hope you didn't?"

"I will next time." He told her about the posters and the memorabilia brought in by white vans with Manchester number plates. And he told her about the toy shop window full of scale models of Charlie's new spaceship. "Has Mr. Atherton given them permission? Charlie designed the spaceship. The copyright is his. And I'm his loco parentis!" But what annoyed him most of all was the sight of five French school children sitting on the steps of the Town Hall and smoking. They were members of a school party on a legitimate educational holiday, and had spent the morning at the site of the county's best preserved Roman villa. The sight of them rankled Grandad because they got in the way, and because he had long been banned from smoking by his do-gooding wife of even more sense than years. 'And-They-Were-Only-Children!'

On getting back home he picked up the telephone and rang a friend in Lyon. With a tone of voice that made no disguise of his annoyance, he said: "Can you look out of the window and tell me if you can see any children... Just do it! Look out the window and tell me if you can see any... See! I knew there wouldn't be. They're all here! Every bloody child in France is here, sitting on the steps of the Town Hall and smoking!" With that he slammed down the telephone. Some days it was difficult being Grandad's friend.

Seeing him huff and puff about the garden, Charlie knew, and Steve knew, and Grandma knew that the SUP Mission couldn't come soon enough.

"Okay, we're ready," said Steve.

"How long will you be gone?"

"At least six months. Up to a year. Give the town time to heal."

Grandma held him close.

They hovered over Horsepool Hill but they didn't land. The police had cordoned a landing spot, but Steve chose not to take the spaceship down. "It'll cause more trouble than it's worth." Instead, they gave an impromptu press conference, projected onto a new kind of holographic screen projected from beneath the spaceship. On the screen, Steve apologised for not meeting the crowd face to face, "but I fear that if we go down we won't be able to get back up again." He and Charlie outlined the itinerary and the estimated arrival times at the Seven Unconquered Planets. "We'll make a free-to-air broadcast from each destination, and from points here and there in between. And hopefully we'll have a film for you to watch when we get back." With salutes and smiles they sent their best wishes. Then they went on their way.

"A salute?" said Charlie, wryly.

"Sorry about that," said Steve. "It just happened."

Charlie, who had copied Steve's actions and so had no grounds for polite mockery, laughed. Steve ruffled Charlie's hair. Charlie opened a plastic box and offered Steve a sandwich.

"From Gran," he said. "We have to eat them. It's the rule."

Steve took a sandwich and bit into it.

"Sun-dried tomato and cheese and a Polish meat. Horse I think."

"It isn't is it?"

Charlie shrugged.

"Well, it's edible," said Steve. They ate the sandwiches in silence.

"Are you ready?"

Charlie nodded.

"If you thought the sound system was good on the last ship, just wait until you hear this. I finally managed to install it yesterday. The separation is thrilling. I could spend the whole day listening to music when it sounds like this." He told the music to play.

Elvis Presley sang of the making of mankind.

"Will we get permission to use the song in the film?"

"Elvis would give it," said Steve.

Officers Adams and Alva were having a mid-morning snack in their patrol car by the green when Spaceship 2 cleared the tree line and took upwards into the sky. Through the windscreen they followed its trajectory whilst making involuntary noises of awe.

"Now that's a sight to tell your grandchildren about."

Alva responded with a slurp of steaming tea.

"You've got to hand it to the man."

The car radio called for Officer Adams' attention. Adams cleared his mouth, responded, and was given a coded message that told him that Steve Atherton and Charlie Ellis had started their mission and would not be home for approximately six months, but their patrol schedule would remain unchanged until advised otherwise.

"Six months? I'll be bored in a week."

"You'd be bored at a Venetian carnival."

After eating their snacks, Officer Adams parked the car outside Steve's house and looked up at the strange diaphanous egg that covered the house and some of the garden. It was a forcefield. Steve

Atherton had installed it and activated a week ago, in consultation with the police, who had agreed to investigate if anything pressed against it for more than ten seconds. "It strikes in self-defence," said Steve.

"Ten seconds," said Adams to his colleague now standing near the egg. "I dare you."

"I suppose one of us should give it a go? Check that the alarm is working?"

"That's a legimate reason. I dare you," said Adams, putting his hand out towards the forcefield, tentatively touching it with a finger, then four fingers, and holding them there for two seconds.

"That wasn't ten seconds," said Alva.

"I never said I was going to do it. I'm the clever one."

"I don't know what all the fuss is all about." Alva put a hand on the forcefield and in half-seconds counted "One-two-three-four-five-six-seven-eight-nine-ten" before snatching it away.

"That wasn't ten seconds," said Adams. "Go on. I dare you."

"You do it," said Alva.

Adams put his right hand on the the forcefield and counted to ten. On the tenth second, a surge of light from within the skin of the forcefield lashed him with a bolt of electricity that knocked him out and briefly set his hair and boots alight. Alva was too shaken to respond in the instant, but on regathering his poise, he extinguished the flames and put his friend into the recovery position. Standing back up, Officer Alva looked guiltily left and right. His face a mask of innocence and concern. Adams started to groan.

Chapter 33

"What do you think?" said Charlie, handing Steve a lavishly illustrated journal.

"What is it?" asked Steve.

"It's my journal."

"The SUP Psalter," read Steve looking at the cover. "Is it a cook book?"

"Yes," said Charlie, acknowledging the bad joke. "I started it two months ago."

"What are all these drawings?"

"They're good, aren't they?" Charlie had filled the headings and margins with inked and painted pictures. "The first letter of each section is illustrated with things that tell you what's in the section, either literally or symbolically. All the flowers and plants are ones in Grandad's garden. I've drawn them from life so they're as real as I can make them. They're the secret ingredients for ginger fizz."

"'And what are these? A lion with a monkey's head? A cockrell with a man's head?"

"'Yes. When I went to Cambridge with Gran and Grandad I saw the Macclesfield Psalter."

"At the Fitz?"

"Yes. It's probably the first great work of English art. Grandad said it was the bridge to the Renaissance from the primitive."

"I'm sure it must be," said Steve, unimpressed. "Where do the monkey's come into it?"

'They're called grotesques. It's just fun and symbolic. We come from apes."

"Pictures of industry and supplication," read Steve.

"That means prayers," said Charlie.

"Why are these men rolling down a hill?"

'That's the cheese rolling festival."

"They ran. They didn't roll. Two or three fell over." Steve turned more pages. More descriptive text, more marvels of grammar, more symbolic pictures. "Charlie, a journal should strive for clarity and honesty, unquestionable honesty. If someone found this a thousand years from now, they would think that lions had monkey's heads."

"No, they wouldn't," said Charlie. "It's just the style. A bridge from the Medieval to the Modern."

"Well, they're very good drawings," said Steve handing the book back.

"It's going to be my masterpiece," said Charlie.

Chapter 34

"Charlie come and look at this." Steve had spent much of the morning looking through an Atherton telescope.

"What is it?"

Steve got up from the seat and motioned for Charlie to sit down. "Don't touch any of the dials. Just look though it." Charlie looked through the glass and could see Grandma and Grandad. He let out a gasp of joy. "They are on Horsepool Hill," said Steve.

"This is fantastic," said Charlie. "I can only see Grandad. He's right on the top of the hill by the thing that tells you where you are. Oh, yes. There's Grandma. She's caught up to him. She's telling him off." He took his eye away from the glass. "That's amazing, Steve!"

"Do you want to see something funny?"

Charlie nodded and moved out of the seat so that Steve could sit back down and adjust the controls. When Charlie returned his eye to the viewfinder he was looking at Officers Adams and Alva. They were chatting with the ice cream man. "It's the policemen. What's funny about that?"

"Look at Officer Adam's hand."

"It's bandaged," said Charlie, frowning.

"I knew he wouldn't be able to resist," said Steve.

Chapter 35

On the fifth day of the half-a-billion mile journey to Jupiter, Charlie looked up from his work to see Steve bringing in what looked like a child's paddling pool. A short series of blown breaths revealed it to be a paddling pool ringed with happy bright pictures of African animals. Steve put it down in the centre of the ship and surrounded it with plastic sheeting. Then he went back to his work area and was soon heard making strange scraping and squelching sounds. Charlie leant back in his chair but, from where he was sitting, he couldn't see what Steve what up to. He returned his attention to his own work, drawing a reversed fox and hound hunting scene, the fox on horseback chasing a hound, and had only just regained his concentration when it was broken again by Steve carrying in two buckets of what seemed to be white clay. Steve had changed out of his clothes.

"What *are* you wearing?" asked Charlie.

"A jock-strap," said Steve.

"A jock-strap?"

"Don't tell me you've never worn one?"

"Of course I *haven't*."

"You didn't wear a jock-strap when you did sports at school?"

"Of course I *didn't*. No one does."

"My, how fashions change," said Steve. "Well, put your book down and come and give me a hand. You might want to use that old shirt of mine as an overall." He nodded at a shirt hanging over the back of a work chair.

"What *are* you doing?" said Charlie.

"Making you a robot," said Steve. 'I watched an old *Star Wars* documentary and this is how they made the casing for C3PO. So, you're going to help to cover me with this moulding clay-thing, and we're going to use the moulds to make the casing for the robot. When we've done the body, we'll do the head. You can give it your head if you want to?"

"No, thank you," said Charlie.

"Well, stop gawping and come and get your hands dirty. It goes on like this. Thick and even."

It took two goes to get the moulds of Steve's body, arms and legs right, and three attempts to take a perfect cast of his head. He said: "We'll use it as a frame to give it a human-shape, but you can add in the intricacies from your designs."

Chapter 36

Jupiter's vastness is beyond human comprehension. Charlie's description that it was "bigger than the sky" was true, it filled all visible space, but it would be closer to the full truth to say that if one stood on Earth and looked into the sky, Jupiter would be more than three hundred times bigger than the sky above. It is more than twice as big as all the other planets combined. It is as big as a planet made from gas can be. "If it was bigger it would be a sun," said Charlie Ellis.

"No," said Steve. "It would be a brown dwarf."

"A brown dwarf?"

"The intermediate stage between a gas planet and a star is called a brown dwarf."

"Why dwarf?"

"Because the people who give names to such things are fans of Tolkien. I suppose they called it a dwarf because it lacks the minimum mass needed to sustain nuclear reactions indefinitely. They're what gives off the light. By indefinitely I mean a few billion years or more."

"Steve, what's the necessary mass of gas needed to become a star?" asked Charlie in a way that sounded more bouncy and forced than natural.

"Well you're pretty famous already and you're not fat but you are full of gas."

Charlie grinned.

"About eight percent of the mass of the sun," explained Steve.

"So our sun is quite big then?"

"It's huge. And there are little suns. All of them bigger than Jupiter."

"Wow," said Charlie, expressively. He altered his tone, so that he sounded more like his real self. "We're looking at the second biggest, greatest, most massive thing in our solar system and we're already talking it down."

In the space between sentences they could hear the camera whirring. "Yes, we're not very good at this science presentation thing are we?" agreed Steve. "We'll cut out the waffle. In fact, we'll scrap the presentation." He walked over to the other side of the room, taking care not to step on a tape measure that was on floor, and he turned off the film camera. He turned off the reel-to-reel tape recorder. "That was so false as to be embarrassing. We won't put that in the film."

Charlie nodded. "I forgot to say the *By Jove* thing."

"Let's be thankful for small mercies," said Steve removing the camera from the tripod. "We'll tidy up a bit and then have a proper look at the King of the Planets."

"At the Roman King of all living things."

"See what makes him tick."

The gas planets, Jupiter, Neptune, Saturn and Uranus, are made mostly from hydrogen and helium and, because you can't really land on gas, you don't really land on them, you arrive within them. They arrived within the planet's orbit a couple of hours ago.

"We are there, Charlie. There. We did it."

"By Jove!"

Steve laughed. Charlie had been waiting to say that for days. He'd chuckled himself almost to sleep when he first thought of saying it. On reaching Jupiter, and parking within an orbit kept by Metis, the first of Jupiter's moons, they opened and shared a bottle of ginger fizz. Charlie sent a private message back to his grandparents. They wrote the presentation script, and they tried and failed to make the presentation film. There was no time for presenting when there was real exploring to be done.

Steve now drove the spaceship down into a red cloud and hitched a ride on a wind that whipped them around the luminous planet from left to right. "Strap yourself in, Charlie. This could get rough."

With a surge of power from the ship's engines, they hopped onto a band of orange wind going in quite the opposite direction. It sent them spinning until, on the third go, Steve brought the ship under control. "It's the first time I've properly used the lateral controls. They need a bit of greasing." He withdrew the spaceship back to the orbit of Metis. He used the moon as a sort-of space anchor, a magnet holding them in a fixed position safe from the pulling pressures of Jupiter. It was there that they had tea and confirmed their plans for the planet.

It has long been observed that Jupiter clouds change colour as they get closer to the core, red being the highest colour, followed a few hundred miles later by browns and whites. The lowest colour, or the colour nearest the core, was blue. "Liverpool at the top and Everton at the bottom," said Charlie. "That's the natural order of things. Are we getting this on film?"

"No, because I could tell from your face that you were going to say something stupid."

"Sorry," said Charlie.

"Have you finished your tea?"

Charlie nodded. Steve cleared away the cups and the film camera. They'd decided first to have a look at the planet's core. "We may as well start by making a triumphant discovery," said Steve.

The readings they were getting suggested the core was made from something heavier than compressed metallic hydrogen. They each wrote down on a piece of paper what they thought it would turn out to be. The winner of their private game would earn an as yet undecided prize.

With the viewing screens now fully open, Steve took the spaceship down into Jupiter, down through the red clouds, down through the brown carbonated clouds of methane and ammonia, and down through the violent clouds of violet water vapour flashing white-blue bolts of electric welcome. They spiralled down through the eyes of storms that raged at speeds beyond our imagination. The ship drove down through all the known colours of light until they were looking at the core of the planet itself - a god's treasury - a sea of molten gold.

"Look at that! It's incredible."

"Is it real, Steve? Is is real?"

"Who would have thought it?"

"Is it really-"

"Yes. Gold... By Jove," said Steve, under his breath.

They were lapping the core and gasping and goshing when Steve Atherton noticed a flashing light on the control planel. He pressed buttons and pulled levers. The ship's engines started to strain. Charlie ran over to the other side of the room and engaged the back-up systems. In addition to these, Steve also turned on the manual controls.

Having incorrectly guessed the weight of the elements at the planet's core, because no one but no one had guessed that it was made from gold, Steve had miscalculated the core's gravitational pull. It was stronger than he thought it was going to be. "Don't worry, Charlie. We can ease ourselves out of here."

With the noise of the engines now rising in crescendo, Steve and Charlie struggled and heaved, and heaved and struggled, like fishermen trying to land a prized marlin, as yard by yard, for more than an hour, they pulled the spaceship away from the magnetised liquid metal and back up through the clouds and out into a clean black sky that was surprised by their reappearance. No one and nothing had ever before seen the treasury of the gods and lived.

Steve and Charlie's relief at pulling the spaceship free from the planet was interrupted by the final flyby of a parade of incoming meteorites and shoals of sharp sparkled dust. "Hold tight." Steve swerved the spaceship left and right between falling rocks before setting it back down, with a bump, on the lunar landing spot.

"Look at that!" said Charlie, as white lights ripped up from inside the giant planet whose embracing welcome to the meteorites was so tight it turned them to gas in an instant.

"And dust," said Steve.

"Wow!"

"The aftershocks will continue for quite some time. You did a good job back there, Charlie." Charlie nodded a thank you. "It was hairy and scary but safe. We could have played bumper car off the meteorites and the forcefield would have held. But each collision would have brought a temporary reduction in our power, and Jupiter had sucked away quite enough as it is."

The dials were on or about forty percent.

"Did we get it all on film?" asked Charlie.

"Did you remember to start the cameras rolling?"

"No."

"Then that's how much we got. And maybe that's for the best. The greed for gold is so extreme that I can imagine whole economies on Earth re-gearing themselves for the single purpose of extraction here, if they knew they could haul enough away to remake the Earth itself in gold. Though that would devalue it of course."

"Steve, we have to film this. We can't just let it go?"

The sky around them continued to explode white from the reactions to the impacts of the meteorites.

"Roll a camera if you wish but I'm letting it go. I need to lie down, digest what I've just seen and learned. We made history again today, Charlie Ellis. The film can wait."

"We have to go back and see the gold again, Steve. And maybe take a little bit? A pint pot? A sample? A barrel full?" To each of which Steve said 'no'.

"There's time enough to explore the planet properly. But let's rest awhile. And Charlie, remember The Argonauts. We don't want Talos on our tail. I'm going to park up then go for a nap."

The miracle of their survival weighed heavily on him.

Chapter 37

With the ship parked on Metis in such a way that its crown was always facing the sun, the spaceship began its necessary recharge before any more exploring could be done. The re-charging took five days, which was less than expected, but a full half-day more saw the power units stubbornly stuck at ninety-six percent and, "that'll have to do. I think we've lost the other four permanently," said Steve. "Are the cameras rolling?"

Charlie nodded.

Steve took the spaceship down on a line perpendicular to Jupiter's equator, and they cruised within sight of The Great Red Spot, the

Méliès-like eye on the Solar System, ever watchful over its subjects and charges, including the planet Earth. Above the eye, they dipped inside a lapping cloud and, in that vermilion sky, they finalised a plan to catch a Jupiter rainbow and film themselves catching it. Suspended outside the ship, and outside the forcefield of the ship, Charlie would take samples of primary coloured gas as they worked their way to within a few hundred miles of the core. "But we'll leave the core alone. We don't want to raise the ire of the god."

"Is he really a god, Steve?"

"He looks like a god to me. And he has all the powers of creation and destruction. We've got to be very careful, Charlie. Jupiter's like a living vacuum cleaner. The power of his pull is such that the ship has to remain on an equal power with it simply to hold still, and that's almost forty percent of our capacity. It doesn't leave much margin for error."

"Ten percent."

"Eight percent, because we're missing the four."

"Oh, yes."

"And we'll probably lose another four. This is very dangerous, Charlie. Are you sure you want to do this?"

"If we can't take some gold?"

"We can't take any gold."

"So show me what to do."

They withdrew to practice in a safe orbit above Jupiter. Suited and helmeted, Charlie practised inside the ship. Gloved with gauntlets, he held a pair of tongs, made from cutlrey, with which he gripped something that looked like a camping flask. Eighteen feet away, a ping-pong ball had been blu-tacked to the edge of a shelf. Charlie stood facing the ping-pong ball.

Steve said: "Okay, give it a go. Turn your forcefield on."

A blue rim encircled Charlie. It pulsed before it thinned and settled. Charlie squeezed the tongs. The forcefield punctured briefly as the tongs extended. A second squeeze from Charlie opened a compartment within the cylinder, from inside of which came a gnashing pair of metal teeth, very much like the double-jaws of the monster in the film, *Alien*. The Alien jaws took hold of the ball and withdrew with it into the cylinder. "Why do the tongs have to be so long?"

"It aids the speed at which they come out," said Steve.

"Why do they have alien teeth? You don't need teeth to catch gas?"

"It's not the teeth, it's the suction tongue. The teeth are cap for the tongue." Steve had re-programmed the forcefield to allow a momentary puncture at a four-inch radial point parallel to the rim of the tongs. In the moments of the tong's exit and re-entry, so quick the human eye could barely register them, the body would be exposed to Jupiterian heat and radiation but the spacesuit was strong enough to cope. He was sure it would cope but, then again, the gravitational force within the planet had proved to be measureably different from the calculations he had made when on the Earth. The difference fell within the safety margin, but if he'd slipped up on that calculation, what other mistakes had he made?

"Charlie, let's spend half-a-day re-checking all the possibilities, and getting the cameras in absolutely the right place so we only have to do things once. When you leave the ship you'll be hit by a side wind going at at least two-hundred-and-forty-miles an hour, but the blast shield round the Imax camera will block most of that from you, and I can angle the ship in such a way as to deflect most of the rest, so the main difficulty will be the gravitational pull from the planet itself. It's going to be quite a tug. The planet will be pulling you with such a force that the support rope will tighten to its maximum almost instantly. If you're not ready for it it'll wind you."

They did the checks. They positioned the cameras. Steve pushed three cylinders through grips sewn into the left arm of Charlie's spacesuit. "If you feel any discomfort, just say the word, or give a signal, and I'll bring you back in. If the worst comes to the worst, which it won't, and the support-line snaps, don't panic. Your forcefield will hold for an hour. I won't have any difficulty tracking you down and bringing you back on board, even if you are swimming in gold. Are you ready?"

"I am."

Suited and booted, Charlie walked to a point on the floor marked with a circle. On a nod from Steve, Charlie raised his right foot and stamped it on the floor. The floor dropped within itself, taking him down to the lowest interior edge of the spaceship. Steve pressed a button on the control panel which released a flap in the skirting board of the airlock in which Charlie was now standing. From inside the flap, Charlie pulled a hose-like attachment and fitted it to a connector positioned near the small of his back. Readings from within his helmet told him that the hose was connected securely. He gave a thumbs up.

"Switch your forcefield on," said Steve.

"It's on."

"No it isn't," said Steve.

"Forcefield on," said Charlie. Charlie's forcefield glowed.

Steve Atherton pressed a button on the control panel. "Forcefield locked and safe." It meant that Charlie could not turn off the forcefield accidentally. "I'll let you go on the count of five. One, two, three, four, five." He pressed a green button. The floor beneath Charlie opened. He was welcomed into the all encompassing embrace of Jupiter.

"*Uuuughhhh.*"

"What was that Charlie?"

"That was me. I just had the wind knocked out of me. *Uuuughh.* The gravitational pull is incredible! I can feel it even inside the forcefield. *Uuuughhhh.* I can almost feel the forcefield being pulled away from me."

"Pulled away? Are you serious?"

"It's holding. But it's certainly being squeezed."

Steve's heart was beating faster than Charlie's. He said: "Okay, take the first sample. Don't rush it."

Charlie took a cylinder from his left sleeve and the tongs from his right. He collected a swirl of red gas.

"Good boy. Do you want to come back in?"

"No!" said Charlie. "I don't want the wind to be knocked out of me again. But please take it slowly. Drive slowly. And be quick."

Steve keyed into the main computer and took manual control of the spaceship. "We're easing down now, Charlie." It took three minutes to reach the brown clouds. "We're there, Charlie. Charlie, are you ready to go?"

Charlie's face was contorted as if he was in pain.

"What's the matter, Charlie?"

"My head's spinning. It's difficult to focus on the clouds because they're moving so fast."

"Do you want to come back in?"

"No, I'm ready with the second cylinder."

The second cylinder broke through the forcefield, collected its sample and returned. Charlie tucked it into his sleeve.

"Is it in?"

"Yes."

Steve brought Charlie back inside, first into the lower chamber where his suit was cleaned of radiation. "Ten seconds more. Turn around. Charlie turn around. You need to turn another circle." Charlie did as he was told. When given the all clear, he detached the hose and it snapped back down into its place in the wall. Steve brought Charlie back to the main room of the ship.

"Welcome back."

Charlie took off his helmet and fell to his knees. Then he rolled onto his back and lay there, groaning. He said: "Did you get all that on film?"

"Yes. Absolutely fearsome. Are you okay?"

"A little dizzy, I guess. I wouldn't get too close, Steve."

Steve grabbed a fistful of tissues. He walked over to Charlie: "I pulled you in because I wasn't happy with the way the forcefield was bending. I don't think it would have increased the blast of radiation you got, if anything I think it probably lessened it, but we need to know. I'm going to pull the ship back to Metis and run a few tests."

"Okay," said Charlie.

Steve wiped vomit away from from boy's neck, chest and chin, and made a conscious and successful effort not to wince at the smell. "There. That's got it all. Take your suit off and get on the medical couch."

"What medical couch?" A medical couch, with appropriate apparatus, including new lighting, emerged from within the floor and from the ceiling of the ship. "The things I do for Science," said Charlie, getting to his feet and peeling open the joins in his suit.

Steve pulled the spaceship back to Metis, and again bumped the landing. The scans of Charlie's body cells found no heat or radiation damage. "Just one more test," said Steve, pulling a hair from Charlie's head. "Ouch!"

"That didn't hurt."

Charlie rubbed his head and wore a sulky face as Steve fed the hair into a machine that gave the all clear. "You're all clear, Charlie Ellis. And may I be the first to congratulate you for breaking about a hundred world records?"

"Did I?"

"Most windy ever spacewalk. Spacewalk furthest from the Earth. Youngest person ever to do a spacewalk. First spacewalk ever inside a planet. Highest point ever reached on Jupiter. And including, of course, the most important record of them all: you are *The First Person Ever* To Visit Jupiter. And you were great."

"Thank you."

"We can do the rest tomorrow."

But they stayed parked on Metis for three whole days, much of it spent developing and screening reels of 70mm film. "See, that's why we're using real film. It's something that's real. It's not just numbers. And look at the quality of that image. Those colours. That depth. That texture. My God, this is going to be a good film. I wish now we'd filmed those meteorites."

"And the gold."

"Take your mind off the gold."

Chapter 38

Steve stood by Charlie's side, watching carefully, as Charlie took the Spaceship upwards, downwards and side-by-side. "You mustn't ever lose your concentration when your hands are on the controls. That's the first rule of man-machine mechanics, be it a car, a plane, a boat, a submarine or a spaceship. Concentrate. Always."

"I will."

Charlie was practising driving the spaceship inside Jupiter because he didn't want to do another spacewalk.

"Okay, pull her out and park her up. I'll get ready."

It was now up to Steve to collect the missing colours. The first gas he collected was yellow, but there was some dispute later, at dinner, whether or not the third sample needed to be redone, for the gas inside the collection tube wasn't yellow.

"It never was yellow," said Steve. "Our eyes misinterpreted the colour. All colours change with distance."

"No, they don't," said Charlie, grinning.

"It's to do with the ossilation of the light waves. It's basic physics."

Charlie remained silent, except for his widely grinning eyes. He knew that Steve had fluffed it.

Chapter 39

Assembling and editing the film footage from the outside and inside cameras, and from the hand-held camera that Steve sometimes carried, took up an enjoyable and productive part of each day. When Charlie was at work, memorising Polish vocabulary or reading the histories of the world, Steve Atherton would assemble a sequence for viewing when the homework period was over. Charlie would give his opinion of the offered takes and make his selection. Then they would work together cutting and layering until they were happy with the final form, or until Steve decided they had worked enough for the day. "Do you see how it makes a good link when you dissolve from this scene to this? The round objects on the right of the screen help to balance the composition. The two shapes seem to mould into each other when the scene changes."

"It's pretty," said Charlie.

"And do you see how this sequence is cut to the music? And how the corridor seems to be unending by the way I've cut it?"

"Yes," said Charlie.

"And the zooms crashing back and forth in this scene?"

"Yes, they're great."

"It's all copied from Ken Russell. We're watching another of his films tonight."

"Another film about music?"

"No, a film about women in love."

Chapter 40

Charlie splashed into the room, a towel more or less around him, and was told off for dripping water on the floor. Steve told him to get dressed and send a message to his Grandmother.

"Are we not doing that free-to-air thing?"

"Not looking like that. Get dressed. Your Gran gets the news first."

This is the message he sent home: "Grandma. Grandad. Hello, it's me, Charlie. We are parked near Jupiter in the orbit now of Ganymede, the moon that's bigger than Mercury and Pluto, and we've discovered that it has two little moons of its own, which means that it's really some kind of planet. We've only been here for a half a day and we've already been able to film one of the famous erupting volcanos. It was absolutely incredible. A hundred times bigger than anything you can see on Earth. What? Steve told me to stop exaggerating, but they are huge. You'll see in the film. Steve's got really enthusiastic about making the film. We've got some amazing footage. Steve says we should have brought even more film with us. We have to be very selective about what we shoot. We'll have some scenes edited together for you to see soon.

We spent last night in a good safe orbit between two of the other big moons. The fire moon of Io and the ice moon of Europa. It was great lying in bed last night and watching them go past. There are lots of little moons too, and they're just great. All different colours and shapes. Jupiter itself is fantastic. It's easy to see why the Greeks and the Romans thought it was the King of the Universe. It is in a way, and it's a good King being waited upon by his courtiers, the moons. With his great red eye he looks out for meteorites that are heading towards the Earth and he marshalls his energies to break them up and keep us safe. We've actually seen him do it.

I've taken some lovely photographs, really really nice ones. You'll like them, Grandma. Steve was so pleased with them that has made me the official photographer. He says I should collect the photographs into a book and get them published when we get back. That's a good idea, isn't it? I know Grandad will be pleased about that.

I've recovered from the spacewalk I did last week. And don't be worried when we send you the film. It wasn't as bad as it looks. We've scared it up a bit for the film.

We managed to collect a Jupiter rainbow, clouds samples of all the colours we could find, except for yellow. Steve got most of them. He says we'll be able to make an art installation from them and sell it for A Million Pounds. But I don't believe him.

We have to sit here for a couple of days until the spaceship is re-charged. Before we got to Jupiter, Steve thought it would take weeks to re-charge but we learned that the ship can draw energy from Jupiter itself. The light the planet gives off is perfectly compatible. Steve says that the technical term for that is *A Bonus*. It means we're ahead of schedule, which we need to be because we've worked out that the ship'll take a long time to recharge when we get to Pluto. Probably a month. We'll be there long enough to build a snow castle.

When we're done here, we'll press on first to Saturn. We've got a great trick up our sleeve for the film bit on Saturn. It was my idea, and I'm not going to tell you what it is, because you'll think it's too dangerous. But it isn't dangerous. I was able to prove to Steve that it would be all right. So we're going to do it. It'll make you laugh... I hope. It will make Grandad laugh anyway.

I haven't had time to do much school work since I came out here, but I've been learning a lot and doing a lot. The one thing I haven't done much of is exercise. Steve has got the treadmill working and will be showing me how to use the multi-gym. He says I need to build up my stomach muscles. He says that's why I was sick. So I'll do some exercise every day and I will be healthy and strong when I get back.

I'm going to do two hours of Polish now. Then we're going to watch a Polish film about the Second World War. It's in black-and-white. What? No, Steve says it's in colour. It's about a horse soldier called Lotna. What? Steve says Lotna is the name of the horse.

I hope you've both had a good week, and that Grandad's talk went well. When the transcript came through I read it straight away. I didn't know the Vikings got to Gloucestershire? I always thought they were East Coast raiders. It's amazing what you can learn when you go looking for it.

Steve says we can all go to Norway when we get back, and look at the Viking Ships there. He says the best time to go is in Winter when we can have the place almost to ourselves. He'll pay for it. He says it will be his treat. He knows Norway quite well. He's been there often. Well, I hope you are both happy and fine. We've conquered a planet; planted the flag inside a little forcefield, and let it go, and we're feeling good. With my best wishes. Charlie."

Chapter 41

The ship healed itself and the adventurers moved gently out of Jupiter's orbit, standing silently together as, all the long day long, they watched the giant planet recede into space and shrink to the size of the moon in the night sky on Earth.

"Wave bye bye. That was great, wasn't it Charlie?" Charlie nodded.

"That really was great," said Steve. "And now we're going to have to pick up the pace if we're going to see Saturn before Labor Day."

"What's Labor Day?"

"The start of Autumn. We need to pick up the pace."

Charlie nodded.

A quiet week of mornings was spent looking through the Atherton telescopes, mostly at the planets they had yet to conquer, but also at the miracles of space beyond our solar system. One interesting column of colour found by Charlie was said to be the birth of a planet. "What you're looking at," said Steve, "actually happened billions of years ago. The planet has probably already lived and died."

"What do you mean?"

"It is so far away, the light from it has taken millions of years to get to where the telescope is picking it up."

"So what I'm looking at doesn't exist?" said Charlie.

"It doesn't exist in this living and breathing time in the form that you can see."

"But I'm looking at it?" said Charlie.

"You're looking into the past at something that has already happened."

"Could we visit it?"

"No."

"Not even if we went fast enough?"

"Not really," said Steve. "If you knew the age of the light carrying the image, and the distance it has travelled, and you travelled towards the light at a speed greater than the speed of the light carrying it, for a greater time than it has taken to get here, then, theoretically, you could. For example, if it was a million light years away, you would have to travel faster than light for a million years to get to see it in the flesh, so to speak."

"Or twice as fast as light for half-a-million years?"

"Yes," said Steve.

"That would be some achievement," said Charlie.

"It would, but a journey to see a planet being born isn't worth half-a-million years of anyone's time."

Charlie spent much of the rest of the day scribbling maths and writing in his journal. At dinner he said: "Steve, what if you're wrong about it all?"

"Wrong about what?"

"About the planet not existing when we can see that it does. I think it is proof that we live forever."

"What is?"

"Looking at a planet being born that burned out millions of years ago. If we can see the planet, and we can, then it goes to reason that in a billion years from now, other people will be able to see us now, talking. Well they could see the Spaceship anyway, if they haven't found a way to see through walls."

"No," said Steve.

"No, they could," said Charlie. "When we are born we exist forever. I can probably prove it mathematically, in time."

"No," said Steve. "We only live once and we only die once. It isn't us that lives forever, only the light or the heat that carries our image, and perhaps the energy that animates our frame."

The meal continued without further discussion. Later, in the hour before sleep, Charlie asked: "When we look through the telescope, how do we know how far away the thing is we're looking at?"

"The numbers on the bottom of the frame in the viewfinder."

"I can see them but I don't know how to read them."

"I have told you."

"I know, but I can't remember."

"Actually, I could probably make some adjustments to make it easier. The numbers are what I call binary cubes, binary numbers cubed, so all you need to do is do the conversions, and remember that under my arrangements, they're imperial measurements, not metric. But the numbers are configured only to take in distance and not time. I'll rig up a system that'll do both."

"So, we'll be able to know what year we're looking at?"

"Yes," said Steve.

"And if you feed that through the computers we'd be able to travel back in time?"

"No," said Steve.

The following day, Steve Atherton tinkered with, and dismantled, many of the non-optical components of an Atherton telescope with the result that he rendered it useless.

"But the good news is, I know where I went wrong, and I think I know what I need to do to put it right. But we'll have to wait until we get back to the Bat Cave to fix it. I don't have the necessary tools here."

Chapter 42

The permanent fixtures in Charlie's bedroom included a work desk that he never used, he always used a pull-out desk in the ship's main room, and a bed in which he took his sleep and naps. He was napping when Steve knocked on the door. "Yes?"

"We're there," said Steve. Charlie got up and went into the main room. Talking with a pointed finger, Steve said: "Don't freak out." Then he opened the viewing screen in the ceiling of the main room. Charlie ducked into a crouch. "I don't like it Steve."

"We're perfectly safe."

They were in the Jupiter-Mars asteroid field.

"I've thought of a fantastic idea for the film," said Steve. "And it'll give us a chance to try out the shuttle."

"Is there a camera on the shuttlecraft?"

Steve nodded.

"I'll stay here. You can close the screens."

"Come on," said Steve firmly. "It'll do that phobia of yours good to see the enemy up close. Put some socks and shoes on. We're taking the shuttle out." Charlie did as he was told.

Steve had intended to treat the first release of the shuttlecraft as a fire-drill but knew it would be more productive to do things slowly, to see every stage of evacuation in action, and to assess if there was room for improvement. The shuttle, larger and more comfortable than its predecessor, with room enough for four fold-down beds, could be entered from four points in the main room of the spaceship. Stamping a foot on the given points on the floor opened an entry chute down which the shuttle passenger slid. The release from the main ship was voice-activated but there were push button over-rides. Charlie and Steve were away from the main ship in less than twenty seconds.

"That was good," said Steve. "Very smooth. Remind me to thank the engineers when we get back. Is the camera rolling?"

"Yes."

A boulder bounced off the forcefield of the shuttle and Steve started counting: "Two, three, four, five, six."

"What's that?" asked Charlie.

"That's how long it took the forcefield to recover from the impact." He pointed to numbers on the control panel, and pressed a few buttons. "When the forcefield is at full strength, which it is now, that number is 100. It loses strength when it takes an impact. Watch." They didn't wait long before another meteorite hit the shuttlecraft. The counter dropped briefly to 98, then 99, then it was back at 100. "An impact, such as these, can't knock the counter down below eighty, eighty-five, but I wouldn't recommend running the force-field at less than sixty percent because, below that, it takes too long to revive, particularly in this environment."

They were hit by another meteorite. The counter fell and rose.

"Why would you run the forcefield at anything less than full power?" asked Charlie.

"The forcefield generates its own power, so you may want to channel that power into something else. For example, if the solar generators failed, we could use the forcefield to power the ship. And, as you can see, Charlie Ellis. We're perfectly safe."

They were hit again. Safely. Charlie started to relax until he saw the main spaceship take a big impact. "It turned it! The impact turned the ship!"

"On its axis, and that's okay," said Steve. "The forcefield works outside the laws of Newtonian motion."

Another asteroid hit the shuttlecraft and bounced away safely.

"That would have hurt," said Charlie.

"I saw it coming," said Steve. "See. There's nothing to be scared of." He was feeling pleased that he had righted the wrong of a past failure. And he relaxed so much that he started to show off a little. He flew the shuttlecraft in and out of the falling spinning boulders.

"Do you want to have a go with the controls?"

"No," said Charlie.

A red light beeped inside the shuttlecraft. Steve pressed buttons to silence it, then, with a look of distaste, he looked out of the shuttlecraft's front window and said: "Damn."

"What is it?"

"Nothing to get too worried about, Charlie. But we're about to be hit by an asteroid as big as a moon."

The asteroid was far away but rolling in at pace and in full sight like a round-shouldered bull. "There's no point in us trying to do a runner," said Steve. "That thing's so big it is going to hit us wherever we run to. Sit tight."

"We won't get knocked to Kingdom come?"

"We might."

The strange thing about the way the forcefield worked was that although they were anchored in a vacuum, and could be moved when submerged in water, a rock the size of Gibraltar wouldn't budge them if it hit them head on. "It'll hit, and spin us on our axis, and it'll roll right over. There are about thirty seconds till impact. Close your eyes if you want to." Charlie closed his eyes and braced himself, shrinking down into his seat. They waited thirty seconds. Charlie uncurled from his crouch and saw the whole sky fill with the terrifying rock. It hit within a few feet of his face with such violence that man and boy both screamed. Then everything went black. And they were spinning on their axis. The lights came on, one by one, then in twos and threes. The rock was behind them. Rolling away. The shuttlecraft had stood its ground. Invigorated and embarrassed, Charlie and Steve laughed.

"The funny thing," said Steve, "is the camera on the outside of the shuttlecraft caught all that head on. When audiences see what we just saw, and they'll see it coming at them from quite a way back, they'll run screaming from their seats. I'm going to dub-out that scream of yours though."

"Of mine? You screamed louder than I did."

"I was just clearing my throat."

The counter read 33, 34, 35, 36, 37. They watched in silence until it reached 100.

Chapter 43

There is companionship in the sounds of industry. Today was a day of much work and little talk. They could hear each other working. Steve had a sewing machine going; Charlie was carving with his penknife. Many hours passed before they stopped for tea, an elaborately English ceremony in which the words *yes, thank you* and *please* were much repeated. The tea break took in a long interlude in which Steve watched Charlie eat six biscuits. Without self-consciousness, as if the act was the most natural thing in the world, Charlie maimed each biscuit in turn by biting off its four corners. He then killed the biscuit with an impressive bite that took away more than half the remainder. "Amazing," said Steve. "Have another?"

"No, thank you," said Charlie, now pouring himself the last dregs of tea from the re-filled pot. When the weak tea was milked and stirred to his satisfaction, Charlie drained the warm cupful in six large and not noiseless gulps.

"Amazing," said Steve.

Charlie put the cup down on the table, and wiped his lips with the back of his hand.

"How are you getting on with your work?" asked Steve. "I've heard lots of strange squeaks and squeals."

"I'll show you." Charlie pushed away from the table. He had spent the day carving wooden tubes and binding them together to make pan-pipes. They were the first pan-pipes he had made though he'd seen a boy make a set at the Scout camp. Putting the pipes to his lips, he blew an air-hollow tune which Steve recognised as *Land of Hope and Glory*. Charlie chose the tune because he thought Grandad looked like Elgar in the film.

"I know what it's meant to be," said Steve. "But I heard air, not music."

"It's a matter of thinning the tubes to the right thickness."

It would amuse many observers, that the technical challenge Steve and Charlie found most difficult, when attempting to conquer the planets, was constructing a set of working pan-pipes, a skill almost as old as mankind itself. The whole adventure ground to a halt for almost a week, not that the spaceship slowed to less than a few handclaps short of its cruising speed of one-and-a-half-million-miles-an-hour, and not that the time wasn't spent usefully. It was a task to fill a transit and to colour a film. Steve worked away on Charlie's birthday present as Charlie carved out and carried off a first tune. "What was that?"

"You know what it was," said Charlie. "It was note perfect."

Steve laughed. "I'll crank the engines in celebration. In the morning we'll be within a day of the only planet in the solar system that can float on water."

"No, it can't," said Charlie.

Saturn is almost ten times bigger than the Earth, but its density is only one eighth of the Earth's so, theoretically, it could float on water."

"No, it couldn't," said Charlie.

"If you had a sea big enough."

"Get one, and show me. Anything else would be rubbish. Non-science for non-scientists. So what are you? Wrong? or a non-scientist?"

"I'm an engineer. That means I'm right."

"No it doesn't."

"Yes it does. I think I win that one. Anyway, we're approaching Saturn from the West. Side on. Did you say you wanted to see if first from above?"

"Yes," said Charlie. "Please."

They changed the ship's trajectory.

Saturn has more than a fair share of galaxy-standard wonders. Its rings are the most celebrated spectacle in the solar system. The best way to see the rings is from above, where their magnificence is complemented by an eight-thousand mile wide hexagonal vortex spinning all the colours of the universe. On seeing the unimaginable glory of the vortex, big enough to fit four planet Earths inside it, Charlie, worn down the tiredness of growing up, had a relapse of awed breathlessness and sat down on the floor of the ship. Steve had an almost sleeplessness night wondering if Charlie was becoming asthmatic, and cursing himself for not equipping the spaceship with the necessary tools and fixes, but those were thoughts for later. Now thirty miles down inside the sheer gas and crystal walls of the vortex, the spaceship hooked onto a surprisingly warm updrift and hovered like a seagull.

Chapter 44

Today was *Moon day*, as Charlie called it during breakfast in the thought that that was a good joke, a variation on Monday. Steve didn't understand the joke because he thought Charlie was trying to speak with a Scottish accent, and because he knew it was Tuesday. Charlie kept forgetting to cross the days off the calender in his room. It was Moon day in that it was the day they turned their attention to Saturn's moons. Saturn has dozens of moons, including two patiently waiting to be discovered. Among the moons studied and photographed by Charlie and Steve were bright Enceladus, with its volcanos spewing ice and looking like a living recreation of a drawing by Saint-Exupery; black-faced Lapetus ("my God, she's gorgeous"); the sponge-like moon called Hyperion; and the potato-shaped Prometheus which, every fourteen hours, ripples and reshapes the 'F' ring of his mother, an activity that will get him into the trouble called doom. Prometheus will be the first of the moons to die. But the moons that Charlie and Steve went to on Moon day were Epimetheus and the two-faced Janus. Every four

142

years, the two moons swop orbits in a sort of astral dance. "We haven't got time to wait for it Charlie. I don't have enough information to work out the exact time of the switch, other than it's probably sometime next month. We're just a bit unlucky with the timing. Have you taken all the readings?"

"Yes."

"And sufficient photographs?"

"Just one more."

"One more. Then let's move on."

"Did you get film of them, Steve?"

"Yes."

"And you don't want to wait for a month?"

"We can give it a couple of days at the most. Then we'll have to move on."

It's clear from photographs taken from our own moon that the best place to look at a planet is from its own moon with the sun at one's back. Encamped on Janus, Steve and Charlie spent a long and lazy day looking at Saturn from the sunroof of the spaceship. Safe within the dome of the forcefield, Steve and Charlie watched while wearing flip-flops, shorts and Hawaiian shirts. Steve wore a straw hat. They were sipping their favourite drinks, when Steve inadvertently killed the conversation by saying: "People would pay a million pounds for this view." To which Charlie's only response, between occasional sips of his drink, was to say "A million pounds?" in a tone which hid his thoughts.

"Yes."

"A *million* pounds?"

"Yes."

"*A* million pounds?"

"A million pounds," said Steve.

Charlie sipped his drink.

The moon called Phoebe circles the wrong way, the opposite way to all the other moons of Saturn. "That's what you'd expect though from the Grandmother of Apollo. Grandmothers do have their own rules."

The splendid grey Mimas, with its indented eye, is every school kid's favourite moon of Saturn because it looks like the Death Star from *Star Wars*. It has the same circular indentation. "But paler in colour," said Charlie, "as if frightened of something?"

"Stage fright about being blown up," said Steve.

"What?" said Charlie with a dismissive frown.

"Think about it," said Steve.

But it was the biggest moon, Titan, on which Steve and Charlie spent most of their Saturn days.

"Is that meant to be a joke?"

"Is what a joke?" asked Steve.

"You said Saturn days and today is Saturday."

Bigger than the planet Mercury, and cloaked by cloudy skies, Titan has all the necessary materials to create life as it is on Earth, or rather, as it was on Earth in the beginning, before The Word.

"No, *after* The Word. The Planets come *after* The Word."

"I'd break it from Saturn's gravity then tow it towards the sun to warm it up and get the hydro-carbons moving, again" said Steve. "Then, to speed things along, I'd electrify the chemical clouds. That would take almost a billion years off Nature's approach. But that would still take too long for us to see real results."

"What's the quickest you could do it in? Theoretically? Create complex life on Titan?"

To Charlie's surprise, Steve gave the not intentionally serious question serious thought and seemed to be doing some mental calculations. Then Steve's face brightened and he said: "Seven days, but I'd need a rest after six." This barely blasphemous answer did not impress Charlie who in this, his first adolescent year, had suddenly acquired a moral streak of almost Grandma-like severity, or priggishness depending on your point of view, so the boy wasn't much calmed by Steve's insistance that he was only joking.

Charlie's innocence meant that his newly deepening religious conviction was vulnerable and thus easily wounded when attacked. Too many attacks, or perceived attacks, before innocence weakens and softens with experience and knowledge, particularly in the deep-thinking young, leads either to a completely closed mind, which is the route of much despair, or a fiery defience which damages the defender because the inexperienced defender's response is disproportionate. Steve knew this. And he knew it would be wrong to take The-Easy-Way-Out which would be to blame Charlie's growing tantrum on the trigger (but not the cause) of a lack of sleep. It was therefore somewhat unfortunate at the day's end, when they journeyed back across Saturn and were circling the astonishing white moon called Dione, that Charlie noticed Steve's face brighten with a Cheshire cat grin. Steve wasn't prone to grinning broadly. Charlie knew something was wrong.

"What's the matter?"

"Nothing," said Steve. He was looking through a monitor at computer-enlarged images of the craters on Dione's rump. The moon's face was smooth but its rump is cratered, which was not how it should be, for the face was the leading edge, the side sweeping through the solar system and bumping into whatever came along. It would be like putting the palm of your hand in an open tin of drawing pins and finding that the pins stick only to the back of your hand. That was the puzzle of the moon called Dione. Something had knocked her the wrong way round.

"Let me see what you're looking at." Steve stepped aside. Charlie looked at the images of Dione. On it's surface, in a crater, was the broken remnants of a machine.

"It was an accident," said Steve, with a grin betraying his air of modesty.

"What do you mean?"

"It was a probe. It was huge. I was trying a new hydrogen power system. This was long before the solar cells. The power system proved to be too strong and much too unstable. The probe hit with too big a thump, and at just the wrong angle, and at just the wrong time. And, in fact, I was aiming at Titan."

Steve Atherton had been responsible for shifting the moon on its axis. "The following year, a NASA space probe took the first proper photographs of the moon so there was nothing I could do to fix it."

"Why not?"

"I'd be found out."

Aghast, Charlie thrust his verbs to the fore. "You mean you *knocked* a moon off its axis, and *altered* an alien environment, and probably did *all manner of harm* which we don't even *know* about yet, and you ran away from your responsibilities, and you think it's *funny!*"

"It was an accident. Don't tell your grandmother."

"She doesn't know!"

"Your grandad does. He thought it was funny."

For the rest of the day Charlie stomped around and sulked around within a high moral air of his own and his grandmother's making. A Little Lord Superior, which would have been amusing had the attempt not been so sincere. But a good thing about boys is that they are rarely able to carry a disapproval through a good night's sleep. A true boy is not one to hold onto A Grudge, the foul-tailed demon that prospers only in the smallest of minds. So when morning came around again, and a young belly had been fed and warmed with breakfast, no further mention was made of Steve Atherton's adolescent vandalism. And a good day was had looking at Saturn and its rings through the eyes of Dione. The sights were captured with cameras, pencils and paint.

Fifteen days passed in Saturn-Land and Charlie and Steve still hadn't planted a flag. "Saturn-Land?"

"Yes," said Charlie. "It means Saturn and the area which contains all its moons."

"And it's got a hyphen and two capital letters?"

"Yes," said Charlie.

"The drawings are good," said Steve.

From Earth, and for many generations after it was first observed, Saturn appeared to have only two rings, A and B, separated by a thin gap now called the Cassini Division. In that gap, and causing the gap, is a tiny moon called Pan. Charlie's idea was to land on Pan and play *Land of Hope and Glory* on pan-pipes as Steve planted the flag. It would give a bit of variation to the film, a gentle musical interlude, and it would be in keeping with the scouting theme of the Earth moon visit. But there was a problem. The pipes couldn't be played whilst wearing the helmet of the spacesuit. Charlie argued he'd be safe inside the forcefield without a suit, with air enough for an hour. After some deliberation, and the test run that took the form of the drinks on Janus, Steve agreed. And Charlie practised.

"Your costume is now ready," said Steve.

"What costume?"

"The costume I've been working on."

"I heard the sewing machine going. I thought you were making something for the robot?"

"No, it's for you."

"I'm not wearing a costume," said Charlie. "Unless you've made me a neckerchief."

"You haven't seen it. It's good."

From a cupboard drawer, Steve took out a leaf-patterned leotard fashioned from green cloth. He held it up and said: "If you're going to be playing Peter Pan, like you insisted, you may as well do it properly."

"I'm not wearing that," said Charlie. "It won't fit."

"It stretches, look." He stretched the cloth. "I've made a hat to go with it. But you'll have to wear your boots to counteract the gravity."

"I'm definitely not wearing it," said Charlie. Steve laughed. "Where did you get the cloth?"

"Your grandmother. There's a whole cupboard full of cloth. I've already told her you're going to do it."

"Well I'm not wearing your costume. Sorry you've wasted your time."

The image of a heavily-booted Peter Pan playing pipes on a namesake moon, framed within the rings of Saturn, proved in time to be the part of the film that Grandma liked best.

Chapter 45

The third longest journey ever taken by man was the one that began that evening from the moon of Pan to the planet called Pluto at the cold inner edge of the solar system. It was a memorable journey for many reasons, the first being that Steve set all manner of records by driving the ship faster than anything that weighed heavier than light. There was thundering and wondering and shaking and smiling as the engines turned and tuned and hummed and sang. "Who'd have thought that light speed was an aria?" said Steve.

"Are we going to break lightspeed?"

"No. We'll stay full within the safe side of Einstein Law because we can. There's a chance we'll use up too much power to recharge or get back if we break the seal. And we don't need to. We don't have to get there by tomorrow." He looked up at Charlie and said: "We're taking our time."

Charlie grinned. "How long till close down?" The moment when the ship reached the intended velocity and the ship's engines could ease off, shut down, recover themselves and let momentum and gravity do the rest.

"A minute. Not much more."

"How much power have we used?"

"Less than sixty percent."

Charlie nodded, then started to float weightless and vertical, and Steve's feet lifted off the floor, his hands still on the controls. Their head hair lifted so they looked like Shockheaded Peter. Steve pressed buttons and the weightlessness was gone.

"I didn't expect that," said Steve. "Just another ten, five, four, three, two, one seconds. And. And. There," said Steve, easing the strain on the engines. "That'll do. That'll do nicely." He patted the control desk. The ship went quiet. They were now cruising at multiples of a hundred million miles an hour. Back on Earth, experts monitoring the expedition thought the ship had exploded.

"I feel sick," said Charlie.

"Go and have a lie down. You're right. There has been a change in the atmosphere because of the changes in gravity. I'll run the unit through diagnostics and tweak the controls until I get it right. If you're still feeling sick in half an hour get into your spacesuit. In fact, it's best if you get into your spacesuit now. It won't take me long to put things right."

The other interesting event came just after the midpoint of the journey, Charlie's birthday. He knew there would be presents from his grandparents, and he knew that Steve would unveil the robot he had made for him. Honour bound, Charlie hadn't even peeked at the human-shaped workings Steve kept behind a dressing screen in his work room. But he had spent many fanciful days and nights thinking about what the robot looked like, and imagining what it could do when fully assembled. Most nights he would enter dreamland inventing conversations and adventures with his mechanical friend. He and his robot righted wrongs and saved a princess. She thought he was a little small to be an Imperial Guard: "I'm Charlie Ellis. I'm here to rescue you."

Sometimes, Charlie imagined himself to be Will Robinson, the robot-owning boy on the *Lost in Space* television show, but these imaginings were less than comfortable than the adventures of Luke Skywalker because Will Robinson had impeccable manners. Thoughts of Will did spur him to try harder to be less pointed, so that breakfast on the day before Charlie's birthday was uncommonly full of courtesy and grace.

"Have you broken something?" asked Steve.

"No, Sir. I'm just being polite, that's all. I'm a model of good manners."

"Good mannered boys don't draw attention to the fact they have good manners."

"Damn."

"And they don't swear."

"Damn isn't swearing?"

"Yes it is," said Steve.

So Will Robinson won the manners game. But Will Robinson's robot, with its flailing arms and school-project design, would be eclipsed in the morning by the birthday present being built by Steve Atherton. Charlie knew that his robot had Steve's own body and a sort of C3PO voice, the perfect English butler. He was with Steve when Steve took a digital recording of the film, and showed him how he was breaking the voice down into its component sounds so that it could be re-built to say anything at all, and he watched him tweak the voice to save it from the god called Copyright.

Perhaps the robot would also be armed? Yes, arming the robot would make sense because there would be times on Earth when Charlie would need a bodyguard. Pleased by this thought, Charlie relaxed into a reverie of advanced weaponry and a shape-shifting robot skilled in the most proficient martial arts. He imagined himself in a buddhist temple, legs crossed, head shaven, a saffron robe around him, as he watched the robot perform an elaborate kata with swords. And then the robot grew several arms, each holding a scimitar. Afterwards, the robot bowed its head to Charlie and called him *Grasshopper*.

Then Charlie remembered talking with Steve about making a kind of Bat Suit, ribbed with wings that would unfold so that the wearer could fly. The idea never progressed beyond an "I'll see", but could Steve have incorporated flight into the robot's functions? Perhaps there were gas jets in his feet? Surely Steve would have moulded in some solar cells? Charlie imagined himself carried above the roof tops, piggy-backed on the shoulders of the world's most impressive machine. Yes, on the morning of his fourteenth birthday, Charlie Ellis would have a robot friend, a best friend who would make all his dreams come true. All he needed now was to go to sleep, dream the dream, and wake again. His dreams were so deep and comfortable that night, full of daring deeds and flights by firelight that, when Charlie woke on the long remembered day of his birth, Steve had almost finished cooking breakfast. The air was thick with the smell of two-by-twos.

"Good morning, Charlie. Happy birthday."

On deep dream mornings, the mornings after heavy nights in dreamland, Charlie's hair stood on end, stiffened with sweat. The sticking-out hair could be used as a sort of barometer to measure how much Charlie was awake. Between each stage of dressing, he would pat the hair down, and it would rise again a little less. More often than not, the hair would flatten itself as Charlie ate breakfast.

"When you're dressed and fed, you can open your presents," said Steve. There were two forty-inch square brown-paper parcels, thin, attached to the wall in the library area of the ship.

"I bet I can guess what they are," said Charlie.

"I bet you can't," said Steve.

"Pictures," guessed Charlie.

"Not really," said Steve.

In the corner of the room, covered with a bed sheet, was the robot. Charlie kept looking at it as he ate his breakfast. His eyes stealing looks over the top of his knife and fork. Then, with the breakfast finished, and the plates cleared away, he said: "What should I open first?"

"Whatever you like."

Charlie walked into the library and pulled the covering from one of the parcels. It was a portrait of Grandma but the portrait moved. She blinked. She moved her head a bit. She smiled. The other portrait was of Grandad. It also moved.

"Wow!" said Charlie.

"They run for fifteen minutes but in a loop so they seem to last forever."

"They're fantastic!" said Charlie, genuinely pleased.

"The idea is taken from Andy Warhol. In the 1960s, he made filmed or moving portraits of almost everyone who came into his office."

"The Factory," said Charlie.

"That's right. But the only way he could see the motion portraits in those days was to play them on a film projector. The only diffi-culty making those was trying to get your grandparents to sit still for fifteen minutes without being self-conscious. They've come out well, haven't they?"

"I love them," said Charlie.

"Now," said Steve. "You can only have your present from me, if you can guess what it is?"

"Any clues?" said Charlie, making his way over to the robot.

Steve smiled. Charlie pulled away the covering sheet.

The first impression was not good. The robot looked more home-made than he'd hoped. The workings were too visible. The face lacked human definition. But the voice was good: "Oh, at last! I thought I'd expire beneath that sheet. You must be Charlie Ellis?"

"I am," said Charlie. "What's your name?"

"I don't know," said the robot, now standing to its full height, a couple of inches shorter than Steve, who had cut bits from the top and the bottom of the legs to make way for the workings of the ankles and hips. The robot was not very steady on its feet. There was an occasional whirr when it moved. "The master said you would give me a name."

"The master?" Charlie raised an amused brow at Steve, who shrugged. "I call you Robot", said Charlie, who was not one for extravagant names. "What can you do, Robot?"

With confidence, the robot said: "I can speak English and Polish."

"Good," said Charlie. "What else can you do?"

"I can recite Shakespeare's play, *The Tempest*."

"Okay. Anything else?"

"I have an in-built library of fourteen music discs."

"Any Elvis?"

"I have his first and his last Las Vegas shows."

"Play them." The robot obliged. As it played the music, it moved its legs and hips in what seemed to be an imitation of dancing. For the first time since seeing the robot, Charlie smiled. Then he laughed. He said: "Thanks Steve. It's a great present."

Chapter 46

Charlie sent a birthday message back to Earth, that included two transmission packages for his grandparents. The first included a lot of technical data that he and Steve had collected and which they wanted to share with the science community. The second was for his grandparents' eyes and ears only, and included two complete film sequences. That was almost a full day ago. By now, Charlie's grandparents would have seen the film of the adventures on Jupiter and the moon of Janus. Charlie and Steve were waiting for the response.

"Do you think they've been able to play the film?" asked Charlie.

"I know your grandmother has played it. She sent me a quick note to say that it had arrived. The bounce signal tells me she played it three or four hours ago. She's thinking of a response. I reckon she's found fault. Brace yourself because she's going to give us a telling off. Praise comes quickly. And this response is not quick."

An hour later, the robot, now monitoring the main computer, said: "Charlie. There's a message coming in from your Grandmother. Should I re-route it to the main screen?"

"Yes, please," said Charlie.

He and Steve sat down.

"Screen," said Steve.

"Lights," said Charlie.

On the main screen came Charlie's grandmother. She didn't look pleased.

"Oh dear."

"Mr. Atherton, I must say I'm very surprised and disappointed, especially after our discussions about safety."

"I told you we shouldn't have sent it," said Charlie.

"Shhh."

"The first film worried me," said Grandma. "Perhaps you've pointed up the dangers and used film tricks to make it seem more dangerous than it really was, but driving a spaceship deeper into a planet of burning gas, when the spaceship was losing power, at a time when it needed more power and not less power because of the gravity, and it was being driven by a boy of thirteen! What were you thinking? If you had died out there, tens of thousands of miles down inside Jupiter, could Charlie have found his way out? Could he have gotten back to Earth? Did you think about that? I'm very surprised, Mr. Atherton. And very disappointed. I hope there's no more of that kind of thing to come."

"Oh dear," said Charlie. "She's not going to like what we're going do on Neptune."

"Charlie. The second clip I liked. The moon and all the colours. I liked the tune you played with it. It was from your mother's jewelry box. It was good of you to remember her. Your Grandad isn't in at the moment but he's keen to see the film. I think I'll record over the first part of it in case it upsets him, or gets him worked up. You know how he can be. He'll like the second part though. So I can show him that. And tell him that's all there was. Tell Mr. Atherton I'm going to give him two clips in return when he gets back. Two clips round his ear hole. So let that serve as notice.

Grandad wants me to tell you that he's giving a talk on the BBC, for the Open University, on March 25th. It's going out live and he'd like you to go with him if you are back by then. They're recording it in Bristol. He was thrilled to be asked. It would be good if you could go with him, Charlie. Well, that's it. Thank you for the film. And good luck with the rest of your journey. With much love to you both, Grandma."

The picture went off and there was silence. Steve and Charlie were both about to talk, and at the same time, so neither talked. Both made the gesture for the other to talk, then both took a deep breath and were silent again. Then the screen came back on. It was Grandma. "Oh, I forgot. I wanted to tell you that the reporting of your mission has been almost constant in the papers and on television. There were some photos of the spaceship at Jupiter, taken by a telescope on Earth. And those pictures have been everywhere. Two of your three broadcasts got through and have been shown a lot. I think the other one must have been lost to the ether. Did you check the numbers before you sent it?"

The screen went off. Then came back again.

"Oh, one last thing. There was a lot of discussion and nonsense in the media when you, what's the term? Cranked it up so you could get to Pluto by Christmas Day."

"Are we going there for Chrismas?" asked Charlie.

"Ssshh," said Steve.

"There was so much nonsense on the television, all kinds of experts claiming that the spaceship had exploded, that I had to telephone in and nip that one in the bud. Unfortunately, since then, there's been such talk about light speed, that the news about you reaching the planets seems to have been forgotten already, or taken for granted. So make the film as good as you can. Fill it with wonder. But be safe." She nodded to the camera in a way that said: 'Don't let me down.'

Chapter 47

Charlie awoke one morning to find Steve standing calmly with his arms folded, his eyes closed, and his ears hosting a stethoscope plugged into an hitherto secret part of the wall of the ship. There was nothing in Steve's relaxed body language and expression to hint that anything was wrong, but his closed eyes suggested a closed concentration, so Charlie left him alone and went to the toilet, into which he took with him a science journal to read, and where he idled at his business. He was surprised on exiting, and completing his dressing that Steve hadn't moved from his listening post. Behind Steve, the robot raised his arms in a manner which said, 'I don't know what's going on.'

Charlie said 'Steve' three times with increasing volume. Steve opened his eyes and took the stethoscope out of his ears.

"Hi, Charlie."

"What are you doing?"

"Oh, just listening."

"To what?"

"The ship."

"What's wrong?"

"Nothing," said Steve with a nonchalance that went against his character and which Charlie immediately saw through. Sensing this, Steve explained: "I often listen to the ship. Usually late at night when you're asleep. It's what engineers do. One's senses are more intuitive than computers."

"So what's wrong?"

"Come here," said Steve, unhooking the stethoscope from around his neck. "Your ears are better mine. You will be able to hear more than I can."

Charlie took the stethoscope: "If anything is wrong you'll be able to see it on the computer."

"Not always," said Steve. "And not at first. The software compensates for faults in the hardware so that the readings on the computer are usually at one hundred percent when, in reality, they're not. Like the human body, the ship's a homeostasistic construct. Tell me what you can hear."

Charlie plugged the stethoscope into his ears, and attached them to the small circular patch in the exposed part of the wall. He listened but he couldn't hear anything.

"Yes, you can," said Steve. "Close your eyes and listen."

"Nothing," said Charlie unplugging the plastic tubes from his ears.

"Okay. How many operating systems does the ship have?"

"Twelve," said Charlie. These controlled the heating and the light-ing, the engines, the forcefield, the air that they breathed, etc...

"Twelve operational systems, all of them different, therefore they all produce different rhythms and sounds. Try again, and see if you can hear a sound that it going 'tum, tum, tum, tum-tum.'" Steve repeated the phrase and clapped it, to give emphasis: "Tum. Tum. Tum. Tum-Tum."

Clap. Clap. Clap. Clap-Clap.

Charlie listened. He could hear it. "I can, Steve. I can hear it."

"Good. That's the main engines. And that's the right rhythm. Now, can you hear one that is going Tum-Tum-Tum-Tum. Tum-Tum-Tum-Tum'. Four identical beats with a slight pause after the fourth."

"Yes."

"Good. That's the air and water re-reconditioning unit. And that's the sound it should be making. Each of the twelve systems has a different beat, or a different pitch. You should be able to hear all twelve. If I can hear all twelve, you should be able to hear them clearly. It just a case of training your ears to pick out each sound in the orchestra of the machine and decipher the threads of the symphony. When you pick out a new rhythm, clap it for me."

Charlie listened and picked out the sounds and clapped a new rhythm.

"Good. That's the rhythm of the heating unit. Spell it out to me."

"Beat-beat-beat-beat-ping-ping. Beat-beat-beat-beat-ping-ping."

Good. You're getting the hang of it. Wire the rhythms into your brain. Give it another twenty minutes or so then do another twenty minutes this evening."

In time, Charlie picked out, clapped, and learned the twelve rhythms of the machine music symphony Steve called A Failing Perfection, including the one that was a little bit different to what it should have been. An irregular pause meant there was a problem. "It means there's a fault with the forcefield. The computers haven't identified a fault because the back-up is programmed to kick in automatically when the forcefield needs the extra power. Without the back-up, it is not hitting a hundred percent. It's cranking in the low nineties."

"What's the critical point?"

"A ten-percent forcefield will deflect seventy percent of the impact of a ton a foot."

"Or less than the bite of a wolf. If the main system goes down will the back-up be able to cope?"

"The back-up is good for forty-to-fifty-percent."

"What's causing the problem?"

"Probably a faulty component in the power unit. Impossible to trace without dismantling the whole unit, and that's not worth the risk while it's still working."

Chapter 48

They were a long way from home. The distance in miles from where they were now, and the point to which they needed to return to, couldn't be counted in seconds in a man's lifetime. They were so far from home that they were looking at things at which no living man had ever looked at before, or would ever look at again without the help of a telescope. They were at the point at which all souls depart to Hell or to Heaven. They were looking at Pluto and at its quick revolving moon, Charon, the boatman to the City of the Dead, "the presence of which is enough to categorise this as a full planet to me," said Steve. "Pluto is the brother of Jupiter and Neptune. The King of the Underworld. It is disrespectful to the Romans to say he's no more than a moon."

Steve walked into the kitchen area, opened a cupboard, and came back with two chocolate bars. He held one up, out of Charlie's easy reach. "You can have this if you can tell me three interesting things about Pluto."

Charlie smiled: "It is smaller than twelve moons including our own."

"Is it?" asked Steve, in a manner that made it clear he didn't know.

"Yes!" said Charlie. "It was named by an eleven-year old English kid from Oxford, called Burney."

"Was it?"

"Yes it was! You really don't know much, do you?"

Steve's attempt to defend himself, or to chastise Charlie's rudeness, was interrupted by Charlie saying: "Can I name a planet if we discover one?"

"*If* we discover one. But I already know what you'd call it."

"No, you don't."

"Planet," said Steve. "You'd call it Planet."

"Damn," said Charlie, grinning widely and a making a mock stamp with his foot.

"No swearing," said Steve.

"That wasn't swearing."

He reached out for the chocolate bar but Steve held it away.

"You've only come up with two improbable facts," said Steve. "Tell me a third."

"Oh, it's *improbable* facts you want now," said Charlie. "A third improbable fact is ... is ... it is the only planet in our solar system discovered by an American."

"Was it?" asked Steve.

"Yes!" said Charlie. "Percival Lowell."

"What about the 1973 thing? That's quite near here, relatively speaking."

"That's not a planet," said Charlie. "It's a snowball."

"It's bigger than Pluto."

"Is it?"

"I think so."

"Are you sure?"

"Not really." He gave Charlie the chocolate bar and opened the other for himself, but Charlie wrapped an arm around Steve's arm to stop him from taking a bite. "Give me that!"

"What?" said Steve.

"You haven't earned it yet."

Steve gave Charlie the bar of chocolate and asked what did he have to do to earn it? He had to come up with three interesting facts about Pluto, but with the added difficulty that each fact he came up with was dismissed by Charlie as not interesting.

"I suppose it's about the size of America," said Steve.

"I suppose you could land it in America, just," said Charlie, "but the West and East coasts wouldn't be covered. Its surface area is much greater, though."

"Is it?" said Steve.

"Yes," said Charlie. "And that's not interesting."

"It's named after the Greek God of the Underworld," said Steve.

"It is," said Charlie, "but - "

"That's interesting."

"Okay, I'll give you that."

"Charon, its moon, was the ferryman in the Underworld who

rowed the dead across the river Styx."

"Acheron," said Charlie. "Styx is Latin, not Greek."

"Is it?"

"Yes,"

"Well, I'm counting that as well."

"Okay."

And on and on they played. The robot, keen to impress and taking it all in, soon thought that conversation consisted of posed questions and a string of denials, with the result that it became very boring at dinner time.

"How do I switch this thing off?" asked Charlie.

"There's a powerpack on it's hip. You unclip it."

Charlie unclipped the powerpack. The robot slumped forward, hit its head on the table, then fell backwards off its chair.

"Was that meant to happen?"

"No," said Steve. "But pull its legs down. It's impolite to keep legs in the air like that."

Chapter 49

"It's cold."

"Congratulations, Charlie. That's probably your most memorable first words yet."

"No, really, Steve. It's cold."

It was minus 312 degrees. Charlie and Steve were standing on the frozen methane crust of Pluto.

"And it's getting colder. Steve! it's biting!" Charlie gripped at his chest. "It's hurting me!"

Steve hurried Charlie into the airlock. There was a lot of activity in the airlock.

"Steve! It's burning me!"

He hurried Charlie into the main room.

"Medical Couch."

"Ouch! Ouch, you're hurting me!"

He sprayed the wound. "Keep still, Charlie."

Needles.

"Try to keep still."

"Ouch!" Charlie's eyes followed Steve's hands.

"Just a little bit more. Just hold still for a bit longer."

"Ouch!" There was tissue damage across Charlie's chest and the low atmospheric pressure had been pulling fluid through the wound. The cold had been eating him alive.

"There must have been a fault with your spacesuit," said Steve, "either a fault with the power supply, or the unit has been damaged."

"Will it scar?"

"I hope not. It's not deep... Is it still hurting?"

"Yes."

"When the pain starts to build again, if you don't mind, I'll give you something stronger to put you to sleep. I'd like to have a proper look at it. I'm sure it has settled down, but I'd like to take a closer look at the recovery pattern to see if I can speed it along."

"When will that be?"

"The first drug will wear off in about two hours."

Chapter 50

Days passed. In his weakened state, Charlie became a little boy again. Gone the rude confidence of adolescence. He became meek and sickly and vulnerable. And that frightened Steve. It frightened him not because he lacked experience for caring for the weak and needy but because it freed the knowledge, locked away inside himself, that this whole incredible adventure was a risk to the life of a child too young to understand the meaning of mortality. Charlie's wound was deeper than had first appeared. Steve calculated he'd been within forty seconds of dying.

Then the boy became feverous. Should we stay? Or should we go? He decided it wouldn't be fair to call off the mission and return home without Charlie's permission. To do so would cause too much psychological conflict down the line. It could tear new wounds that would be difficult to heal. He didn't think it would be right to ask Charlie until he was sufficiently recovered to think through an answer. And the ship needed time to recharge. He rigged up a temporary round-the-clock monitoring of the ship's external forcefields, which he re-routed to the transport controls so that, at the first real sign of weakening, the moment when the software failed to compensate fully for the fault in the hardware, the ship would take itself home. This brought Steve some comfort. It increased the time he could spend at Charlie's side. And it gave him more time to look for the cause of the failure of the spacesuit.

Days passed.

He opened his veins in the laboratory.

He fed the ship.

He fed the new flesh.

He dreamed that he was Charon.

Chapter 51

The screen came down and a French film played, *Les quatre cents coups*, about an unloved boy who runs away from home. In the circumstance of a slow and uncertain relief after the crisis of Charlie's injury, and continuing illness, it wasn't the wisest choice of film to show, because the mood on the ship needed lightening. Throughout the screening, Charlie was attentive and silent from his viewing place propped up from the medical couch, and, in the quiet moments before sleep, and on waking, he found himself going deeper into himself than is sometimes wise. He asked him-self the questions of who he was, and of what he was going to be, and of how he came to be, and it took Steve careful days to shake him from his introspection.

"Steve?"

"What?"

"What's your first memory of me?"

"I remember you before you were born."

"No, you don't."

"I remember touching your mother's stomach and feeling you kick. She loved to show you off. I remember her saying to me 'Feel how he kicks. He's so full of life he can't wait to be born.'"

"You met her on her first day at university, didn't you?"

"I'd met her at your grandparent's house. Once. Three or four years before that."

"Just once?"

"Once."

"She's younger than you isn't she?"

"By a year. Early in the first term of my second year at the university, I was looking through the class lecture list pinned to the wall outside one of the lecture rooms, and I saw your mother's name. I knew it was your mother, and not just someone with the same name because, by the names, not just hers but by everyone's, they'd printed the name of the school they'd come from. I thought that was a bit odd. I was surprised there was someone from a school near to where I lived."

"My old school?"

"That's right."

"Did Grandad not tell you she was studying at the same place as you?"

"No. I sought her out and said *Hello*."

"Did she remember you?"

"She said she didn't but she did."

"Was she clever?"

"She was very clever."

"As clever as you?"

"She... erm... didn't work as hard as I did; at least not as hard as I did when I really began to get a feel for the subject."

"What do you mean?"

"Well, for the first couple of years we were very close, very good friends. Inseparable, in a social sense, in that we socialised together. We didn't study together. We weren't doing the same subjects. Things changed when the subject I was studying got easier for me."

"What do you mean?"

"Almost over night, I seemed to develop an ability to read mathematics as if it was my first language. I could solve formulae as quickly as I could read or write them. And that was very seducing. It opened up new worlds, inside of me. With the result that I'd spend more time in the labs than I'd spend with your mother."

"And that's when she met my father?"

"I don't know when she met him, but I didn't meet him until, I think, the second term of my final year. I didn't really get to know him until the year we left. I'd heard about him before I met him."

"Why?"

"He was a popular fellow. Everyone in college knew who he was."

"He was College President, wasn't he?"

"Possibly, I don't know for sure; college politics never interested me and I never attended formal dinners, but he probably was. I know he was high up in the rugby club."

"Was he good at sports?"

"Obviously."

"Better than you?"

"Obviously."

"I'm not so bad."

"You're okay."

"What did you think of my dad?"

"He was okay. I didn't really know him all that well, Charlie. I probably only talked with him a dozen times in his whole life. His conversation was mostly sports."

"Can you remember the first time you met him?"

"Your mother introduced him to me."

"He told me he thought you were going to hit him?"

"Did he?"

"That's what he said?"

"I can't remember that. I'm amazed. That's a very strange thing for him to say. I'm surprised at that."

"Why did you want to hit him?"

"I really can't remember."

"Yes, you can."

"I do remember being surprised to see him. That much is true. Meeting him was quite a surprise at the time."

"What do you mean?"

"Well, it was just so soon."

"Soon?"

"It was no secret that your mother and I were very good friends. As I said, we were inseparable."

"Inseparable?"

"It means *always together*. For example, at the end of our first term, the Christmas term, your Grandad came to collect your mother and take her home for the holidays. That was when your Grandad had a beard. You've seen the photographs. I knew your Grandad, of course. He had paid for the last two years of my schooling, and he gave me that lab at the mill in Roeminster when I wasn't much older than you. You know the kind of man he is. He gives money to worthy causes. When he collected your mother from college, he thanked me for looking after her, which I thought was a bit strange. Your mother was not a woman who needed looking after. He seemed a bit embarrassed that there wasn't room enough in his car to take us both home, you know, drop me off at my mother's housee. He knew I didn't have much money. Your mother always had so much stuff, so many bags. I think he was a bit embarrassed that he was rich and I was poor. But I was staying on at college for another week or so, in any case, so it didn't matter."

"You were poor?"

"You know I was poor."

"Is that why you didn't marry my mother? She told me she'd asked you to marry her."

"She told you that?"

"Yes, and in front of Dad."

"That's very naughty of her.

"They were having a row."

"That was wrong of her to say that."

"My Dad already knew. Was it true?"

"She did ask me to marry her."

"And you said no?"

"Yes."

"Why?"

"I didn't think she was being serious. Marriage wasn't in my thoughts at all. I was too busy being brilliant. Too brilliantly selfish."

"She married Dad when they were still at university, didn't she?"

"In the college chapel. And you came tumbling out soon afterwards."

"I couldn't wait to be born. You said so yourself."

"I know. You were a lovely kid."

"I still am."

Steve ruffled his hair.

Chapter 52

Steve discovered that the hole in Charlie's spacesuit, about the size of a small coin, was caused by the gold St. Christopher he wore around his neck. "It doesn't make sense, I know," said Steve. "But gold does have unusual properties. Who'd have thought it could dismantle the electronics in your spacesuit? That's something we're not going to put in the film."

"You didn't film me throwing up, did you?"

"There no film at all of your sickness."

"If gold is the problem," said Charlie. "Think of Jupiter?"

"We did well to leave the bounty alone." He mopped the sweat from Charlie's brow. "I'd like you to get up today. And sit at the table and start eating proper food again. You'll find it hard at first, but you've lost a lot of weight. It's important you start eating properly."

The St. Christopher discovery initiated a gold hunt aboard the Spaceship. Everything gold was stripped away and ejected. There wasn't much: three books decorated with gold leaf; a fountain pen; seven electric coils, a pair of cufflinks patterned with the crest of Steve's university, and Charlie's medallion.

"No gold teeth?" asked Steve.

"No fillings at all," said Charlie.

But Steve neglected to remember that gold was used in the alloy from which he'd made some of the circuits inside the robot so that, in time and in all innocence, the robot wore away the ship's defences. But that is getting ahead of the story.

With the forcefield now extended outwards from the spaceship to cover an area seventy-five feet long and seventy-five feet wide, and with Charlie sufficiently recovered to be wearing the spare space-suit that used to be kept inside the shuttlecraft, Steve and Charlie stepped out onto the surface of Pluto to plant the flag.

Stepping out after them, and showing much tredipdation, is the robot. The robot is wearing a fur-hooded eskimo coat. It stands mute and puzzled as Charlie and Steve laugh at it. Charlie plants the flag. "Four down. Five to go."

"Four?"

"Grandma said we've conquered the Earth."

"I suppose we have."

"We're the kings of science."

"You are, Charlie. I'm an engineer."

"And a doctor. Steve, you said we could build a snowman at Christmas?"

"You missed Christmas, Charlie."

"Did I?"

"It's February. I'm sorry."

Steve turned away and walked back to the spaceship. He didn't look back. Charlie watched him enter the ship and close the door. In the airlock, Steve tapped solid methane from his boots and watched the still visible gas exit through the extractor.

Outside the ship, Charlie tried to roll a snowball.

Chapter 53

"Is the universe expanding?"

"Some of it is, and some it isn't. It's going in and out, in and out, all the time, because it is the lungs of God. We are like Jonah in the belly of a whale."

END OF BOOK ONE

www.ingramcontent.com/pod-product-compliance
Lightning Source LLC
Chambersburg PA
CBHW030753200726

48288CB00004B/1147